I0647746

Also by John Antrobus for BearManormedia

THE MILLIGAN PAPERS

Six BBC Radio Comedy Scripts
(The last Radio series Spike Milligan did for the BBC)

THE HORSE MUTINY
The stories of three horses in World War One.

Due out for Christmas 2020 !!! Don't miss...

GOON BUT NOT FORGOTTEN
Mad encounters with Super Goons Spike Milligan and Peter
Sellers, including the TV sketches John Antrobus wrote for
them...
And how on earth do Sherlock Holmes and Watson become
involved in the pages of this book?

INVITATION TO A PLAGUE

by
John Antrobus

BearManor
Media

Orlando, Florida

Invitation to a Plague
© 2020 John Antrobus. All Rights Reserved.

No portion of this publication may be reproduced, stored, and/or copied electronically (except for academic use as a source), nor transmitted in any form or by any means without the prior written permission of the publisher and/or author.

Published in the USA by
BearManor Media
1317 Edgewater Dr. #110
Orlando, FL 32804
www.BearManorMedia.com

Softcover Edition
ISBN: 978-1-62933-603-9

Printed in the United States of America

INVITATION
TO A
PLAGUE

1968

CHAPTER I

Inspector Hedge was unused to the heat in the Police Canteen. Though he wore a knee length tunic and toupee - it wasn't bad for Fulham Broadway in February. He worried much about promotion - although he called himself Inspector Hedge and was paid as an inspector and indeed given an inspector's work - he was sure they all regarded him as a sergeant. This made him nervous and snappy in his work - and once he bit the constables at the gate. The constable was a likeable chap and reported him.

It's the heat, sir, Hedge explained to the Superintendent who idly sat watching the blizzard outside his window.

I'll give you a shilling to clear the snow from my car, quipped the Super merrily.

Don't be like that, sir, said Hedge. To be honest I think I'm sickening for something.

Which is why I've called you here, said the Super on a serious note. You may have noticed there aren't many sick men in the force – I mean sick in the head. He ponderously tapped his head. You see, continued the Super, there are jobs to do - catch a crook to catch a crook.

<u>Set</u> a crook to catch a crook, corrected Hedge.

That's the chap - see here Hedge - the man we want is very sick unbalanced - a hell of a mess - a menace - a loony - powerful - unhinged - Frankly, you're the man for the job.

Who, sir, said Hedge.

We don't know who - we hardly know where - it'll need a right nutter like you to sniff him out.

What's his game sir, enquired Hedge on a serious note. And could I have a glass of water please?

Certainly.

The Super fetched the glass of water and Hedge put his teeth into it. Thus relaxed he addressed himself to the task ahead.

Now pay attention, said the Super. Here I have a map of Britain - on it are all the Bonzo petrol filling stations in the country - does that mean anything to you?

No sir.

Just a shot in the dark.

The Super tore up the map.

Just a minute, said Hedge. Isn't Bonzo the new barking petrol. You're never alone with a gallon of Bonzo Woof Woof.

Indeed it is, sighed the Super. So much so that motorists all over have been sighted chewing dog biscuits - a sympathy syndrome.

Never mind that, said Hedge.

We won't - now pay attention.

At this point, Hedge's teeth clicked shut in the glass - audible throughout the room.

Why did you take your teeth out? Asked the Super.

Hedge glumly grinned.

I see. Now pay attention, Inspector. This petrol company Bonzo has been fouling up the highways with its barking petrol - the din on the M.1 is incredible - a joke is a joke, but...

Do you ascertain some serious menace behind this, said Hedge, eyeing the Super coldly.

The Super dipped an idle finger into the glass and toyed with Hedge's teeth.

The problem is to get a strain of petrol which gives an Alsatian bark - given that the whole Force would go Bonzo.

Hedge felt he was being tested and grinned. He had a moment of clarity. It was something to do with the medication he was on.

What are you smiling at Inspector?

You want me to call you mad, sir - so that I disorientate. But you are well. I am feverish. I have one question to ask. Are we here? Are we real?

That need not concern you, said the Super. All you need to know is that you are the man for the job.

Hedge was sweating.

He was looking for clues already. It could be in the set-up. After all the Police Force was a series of scenes, wasn't it? You had to get hold of a story. 'This story of yours ' that's what they said. But they didn't say

' This story of ours ' because without a story you were sunk. Hedge needed a story. More than anything else, that's what he needed. Or he was stuck - in a revolving door - with his Superintendent.

Now pay attention…

The Super was coming in and out of focus. Concentrate. Breathe.

And then the Super unfolded a most strange plot.

It appears that…

Ah, we're getting to it, Hedge gasped. It appears. It appears. We have an appearance…

Are you married Hedge? Shot the Super

No sir - currently void to that state though my Mother was married.

That's a curious answer...

It appears that in a private nursing home…

I can visualise it, said Hedge. The grounds. The building. The barbed wire fence...

Did you hate your father? Asked the Super.

No more than I would hate the ordinary man in the street, replied Hedge. And you know what pigs they are.

A murder has been committed in this nursing home.

Do you believe in dreams, sir? asked Hedge.

You are interrupting me, said the Super, and it just so happens I do.

Well sir, I was in heaven last night - and all the Angels had been plucked and stuffed for Christmas - rows of them hanging upside down stuffed with sausage meat - I thought I'd best report it.

It may have been an apparition not a dream, said the Super thoughtfully. We should send someone up there to check. When you die you will go straight to heaven. That means you must lead a blameless life, Inspector.

Order are orders, said Hedge also thoughtful. I've always been a good policeman. Methodical. To be blunt, sir - as is my way, for what it's worth - I am having trouble with this scene.

Are you. Then let's get it out of the way. Now pay attention. There has been a murder in a nursing home.

National Health or private?

You can't get murders on the National Health, Hedge.

They laughed for some time until the Super said, That's enough of the laughter.

But still Hedge continued chuckling. The Super struck him on the wrist with a ruler.

I did that for your own good, man. This murder has taken place in an isolation ward.

Good idea, said Hedge.

It is an incurable ward. All the inmates will be dead within a fortnight.

Good show.

Some strange bug, Hedge - code name Green Swan - but one of them has been murdered already.

It doesn't matter, sir! Hedge roared with laughter. It's all over bar the shouting for the lot of them.

Stop this merriment, said the Super firmly though his eyes twinkled. How would you feel if one of those men in that ward had been your own mother?

These... these... these...

Incurable, supplied the Super.

Well what's it matter if they go round killing each other - in extremis absurdum...

Be that as it may, said the Super , and I'm not sure it's Latin - we have a job to do. That's why we're paid.

And have a good pension plan, sir.

The Super leapt to his feet and Hedge stood on his chair. They sang God Save The Queen but to some strange Gregorian chant. That's the way it is in the Force. Hedge dried his teeth and replaced them into his mouth.

I've not enjoyed myself so much in years, he said.

The moment is brief and life is short, said the Super. He handed his inspector a file.

In that file you will find all the details you require and forms to fill in for your expenses which do not include my Christmas gift.

Perhaps God was angry with them.

Who?

The Angels, sir.

God has got a lot to answer for, said the Super.

Or our idea of God must change, replied Hedge.

True, Inspector. But meanwhile we have work to do on earth. Let us concentrate on that.

CHAPTER II

It was wonderful to be out in the country. Inspector Hedge removed his toupee. Where was he? He consulted his Bonzo road map of petrol filling stations.

Here I am, he pondered lightly. Yes, here - sitting beside the map.

He made a note of his position.

I am sitting on a grass bank where crickets sing beside my Bonzo map, he wrote.

He stared at the note and then ate it. It was silly to take chances in the heart of Surrey. It was possible that Japanese snipers had still not surrendered. Besides it would soon be dark. He took out his inflatable rubber policewoman and blew her up. It seemed ages ago that he had decided to abandon the police car and strike out across country with her. thus he had gained the element of surprise though who he was to surprise he had not the faintest idea. For he had left his case file in the car, a wanton act of forgetfulness. Or rather a hunch that he was better to find his own way in this strange case.

I don't give a damn, he thought. And overcome by lust he seized her the inflatable one, the familiar scent of rubber in his nostrils. Do you realise, he muttered, that were it not for my regulation issue bicycle pump you would be nothing to me?

Having satisfied his lust with this display of verbal fireworks he lay back and thought about his father. Fate had been cruel. Father had been a sea captain of a passenger liner. However under the influence of Marmite shortly after leaving Southampton he had fallen into the habit of shouting, Women and children first! And ordering them into the lifeboats, meanwhile sailing on to New York. There was no emergency, collision or fire, but he protested at the various enquiries that it was better to be safe than sorry. That was his story anyway and it was true that he had been retired suffering from over-anxiety. He took to ringing the bell on London Transport buses between stops. He had the good sense to desist from shouting, All change! Women and Children first! And instead his slogan now became Keep Enoch Powell White! He was reported to the race relations board for attempting to inter-marry with an Irishman on the Circle Line. He claimed that he was under the influence of Victor Mature in the film The Robe and the Home Secretary paid both their fares and had them deported to Putney where they went native and shopped locally. Of course the story could change like the weather, it was hard to pin anything down.

The sun was still warm on that summer evening and the inspector was loath to move on. I wonder what it's like to be incurable, he thought. He had been to the doctor recently who had only given him fifty years to live and advised him to make the best of it. Which was why Hedge was so lighthearted these days.

He deflated his prospective rubber policewoman and prepared to move off into the dusk. Once he had taken her to the Serpentine and created a sensation by floating on top of her. Another time he had overin-flated her at the Police Ball in a moment of madness and ascended hanging on to her legs. He had been sent on a month's compulsory sick leave and had his puncture repair outfit confiscated.

He spied a teenage property developer through the bracken. Inspector Hedge tensed as he felt for the handcuffs. Yes, there was the lad measuring out his footsteps. He leapt out to confront the lad!

Have you got planning permission?

What for, replied the lad innocently.

A block of flats.

I think you must be mistaken, said the pimply faced youth. I was just taking an evening stroll - actually I'm a sex maniac.

No excuses now, tempered Hedge.

The lad slipped from his grasp and fled into the gloom. Hedge stumbled after him. He desperately needed unfurnished accommodation. But soon he gave up the chase. he would put an ad. In the paper - a plain-clothes ad. - using one of his aliases. Then he remembered that all his aliases were on leave. Organisation had never been his strong point.

He blew his whistle and somewhere in the dusk a constable answered. Hedge recognised the call as negative. He was already promised. And night fell between them.

CHAPTER III

When Inspector Hedge awoke the sun was shining and nearby was the police car. He had collapsed and slept on the roadside verge. Where was the grassy bank? A fleeting memory if memory could be trusted. All around him lay the soft dewy countryside.

Ohh mate, said the Inspector, trying to concentrate on a part of his body that did not ache.

He reached in the car for the case file labelled,

CODE NAME GREEN SWAN.

Inside the concertina file was a banana marked, Breakfast Day 1, Love Super. PS Don't slip on a banana skin.

The Superintendent had confidence in him, in his madness to solve this case. Set a sicko to catch a sicko, he had told his inspector. Or implied it. Or not. Whatever the case may be... But he was well. An acute intelligence was at work. He would outwit them all. But who were they?

What is this bug? he thought. What is this bug - code name Green Swan - that is laying waste to grown men?

CHAPTER IV

The nursing home was in the heart of the Surrey countryside. Doctor Fettle loved the garden. He loved the garden so much he hated it. Sometimes it was too much for him. For instance with care and love he would plant peas in the vegetable section and tend them for months till they grew into strong and healthy plants. But then he would tire of them, when it only needed a fortnight for them to be in pod, and nothing could constrain him for he would thrash and beat the plants to the ground and lay waste the area. He was a man of strange moods. One day it was his ambition to plant a tree but the peas were a lesson to him and he hesitated to take this big step. Could he constrain himself for thirty years? It was unlikely. Doctor Fettle was in the army during the war. He was frightened of civilian bombing and thought it would be safer to be with the armed mob up the front. He refused all leave convinced that London was devastated At one point he had believed that London was occupied by the Germans and that they were victims of a gigantic propaganda machine. Letters from his mother he dismissed as forgeries or brain-washing. When victory came at last and they told him he was being sent home for demob he told them he'd had enough and someone else could launch the Third Front. He opened up a small practice in Berlin and braved a day trip to Dover in 1951. Most of his fears were secret and not many people knew of his foolishness. Mother mainly, who died in 1953, leaving the way clear for his triumphant return to Croydon. He was interested in psychological aberrations of war heroes and had soon carved a niche for himself in the old country. He loved playing gramophone records and had a marvellous collection of 78's. An occasional 45 he could listen to but a 33 (those LP's) drove him mad. He had no time for them.

The third of February noted Inspector Hedge from one of the calendars he wore. He always trusted the one he wore round his neck most because he could mark it without doing a cartwheel. But there was no calendar. There was no date. There was no day. Not any more. He was divorced. He felt his pulse. Yes, it was going strong. The rhythm of it all nearly drove him crazy. Beware, Inspector...

What was this strange mysterious all absurd bug he was investigating? He could not arrest a bug. Oh no. On that he was quite clear. How wonderful to have a lucid mind, especially at that time of day or night or day or night or day or night but the warmth of the sun was reassuring. Inspector Hedge checked his watch. Yes it was still strapped to his ankle for reasons of security. He checked his ankle. Yes it was. You'd have to be up early in the morning to be up early in the morning.

He broke through the undergrowth. He thought, I should stumble here... Sort of out of the under-thing grasping for words lost to him his mind a jumble really I should be on sick leave. He tried to stumble. But was too self conscious to carry it off. he had work to do.

There before him was the nursing home. Somewhere. But where???

CHAPTER V

Inspector H. Stumbled through the... oh well he had learnt to stumble pretty well. Soon he should break through this stuff which his limited vocabulary forbad him to name. Meanwhile his thoughts carried him back to his childhood. Misty windows. He had always looked in from the outside. Even into his own. Thought, I should be sitting in there having my tea... Then gone in late and got hell.

Oh he'd just have to go on. He could call it foliage. Or bendy stuff that clawed at him to hold him back. Why did he become a policeman? Why oh why? Some vague hope that one day he might be able to arrest his father. Long since dead. There was always God. And that angel bit. To die and to go to heaven - and arrest God. What a scoop. After all he'd done to Jesus I mean there were grounds for suspicion. All Inspector Hedge needed to bring him in...

And God came back to earth again not as the Son Incarnate but on sus - I'm taking you back to earth God - why should final judgement be in heaven - bring 'em down to earth - here was where it was at! All the apparatus of the law...

His mind wandered. He supposed it was his own. Ah, my dear Inspector - Inspector dear - roving this plane. making the occasional arrest. I now pronounce you constable and criminal. Those were the days my friend. Loneliness. Cold comfort. God is love. You can't arrest love. There were tears in his eyes.

CHAPTER VI

Doctor Fettle looked through the observation glass panel at his incurable patients upon whom depended his living. Morgan waved. Morgan. He of the rubber squeaking grapes. And there was Heartfelt - suffering.

Lambs. Lambs to the slaughter. The bad shepherd they call me.

Fettle laughed.

In the valley of need will Thou comfort me - Thy pill and Thy syringe...

And there was Harbour. Alan Harbour. The youngest of the Incurables. The baby. And yet he seemed to care less than the others.

And there was Fletcher. Black Fletcher. Or coloured Fletcher. From the Colonies. Educated? A scientist? Or lab assistant? Don't jump to conclusions. He the inspector was from the pigs, wasn't he? The trough!

When would the inspector arrive? To solve this gristly murder. It was a party that had gone on quite late and when he, Fettle, had arrived... Oh, that story would wait...

Inspector Hedge did not believe in surgery. That is he did not believe there was anything in his body that could be separated. All this nonsense about heart kidneys lungs etc. There were no such things. It was propaganda. An excuse to get at you and cut you up. After all if they did not name it how could you worry about it? How could you? How could you worry about a heart condition if you didn't know you had one? And they say that worry causes heart trouble. Worrying about the heart. It was all nonsense. Nevertheless he would have a checkup. At the nursing home. Perhaps off the record the Doctor Whatsisname would. As long as there was no surgery nonsense. He didn't want to be told he had a defective heart. Might as well tell him he had defective molecules. A molecule was a molecule, neither good nor bad. If anything existed they did - in all things which was the opposite of separation. A molecule was a particle of energy. That's what we were, energy!

They put a spell on you, man. If you let them. The National Health Service was a religion. We were all supplicants...

But the power of the law would prevail. He, Hedge, Inspector Class 2 merely wanted to be told he was well - or - not so well as he might be - if he had a pain - slight - in his back - yes he had a slight pain in his back - that it was not liver and they were not going to take it out and show it to him to prove it - anyone could cut bits off you and give 'em names - no thank you - Law will prevail!

Inspector Hedge believed in health. Weight lifting and that. And he often carried his weights with him. Even on cases. Which exhausted him rather and he therefore became too tired to do his exercises. To hell with it. Hedge knew it was a heresy but he really believed he had no heart, liver and kidneys...

He wasn't having any mucking about in this nursing home get that straight. He was going there strictly on business. And if they thought they was going to do any of that surgery lark on him they could think again. A bit of a check up - yes. Off the record. But no bits cut off here and there...

He was going on a case. A murder. And he didn't plan to have bits and pieces chopped off his body while he was about it, call it morbid fear if you like...

He had a warrant. He was not a patient. Not a patient. He didn't ask for special treatment. But respect for the cloth. His uniform. Fresh air was the answer. Not surgery. And he was getting plenty of that on this case. A startled bird rose into the sky. A British bird! Now his father, Hedge, had a book, The Book Of British Birds. Also The Book Of British Trees. And The Book Of British Flowers. They were all British, that was the point. National Front nature!

He was hopelessly lost in this British landscape, don't let the Japanese plants in they'll take over. Dad was right. Lost he was. Part of his method. They couldn't know his plan if he didn't have one. Sort of random sample was what he'd call it. A sample experience which contained its own ingredients. Not to be confused with real life, something he had seldom felt - felt that is was happening to him.

He would come across them - whoever they were - he would recognise them. It would come to him in a flash. These are the geezers I am after. A much more reliable method. The Inspector Hedge way of doing things. Meanwhile where the hell was he?

Doctor Fettle by contrast had little respect for the law. Not in this case. Not in the Incurable Ward. What was the point?

The body is one and indivisible, muttered Hedge as he lugged his weights through the undergrowth. Time I had a bit of a stumble, he thought. And fell to his knees. This case wasn't easy. Why did he burden himself? Returned to the police car he had taken his weights. Drop them, lad! Let them go. Let go for God's sake...

Nerves he did believe in a bit. Hedge. I am Jack Hedge. I suppose it was nerves. His mother had nerves, no it was his grandmother on his mother's side. She always carried a bible and blessed people who swore at her. Or was it fear? Of course it was fear. But big policemen aren't frightened - even of the dark. It was nerves. You could go off sick with nerves but then they'd get you - the doctors. And start naming parts. Not only parts of the body. Parts of your mind! Oh dear. The ego, the id, as if he didn't have enough to worry about. Better to be frightened and stay on the job. With your ego and your id. No nervous breakdown - rubbish - that was sheer panic. So - just panic - and keep at it. How could he use his illness - but he wasn't ill - the Super has said so - use it for the job he said. Set a sicko to catch a sicko...

Not that he, Hedge - I am Inspector Hedge - not that he was scared. A little nervy? No! He would not believe in nerves either. He wanted to be quite straight in his mind before he met the doctor. This Fettle fella. He was going to strike nerves from his vocabulary. So's he couldn't be got at that way either...

He was sweating now. British sweat. Birds emigrated from Africa didn't they? In the Spring. That would have to stop. British birds made in Britain, alright Dad? Nesting in British trees! None of your foreign rubbish, keep that in Kew Gardens and make sure it didn't escape. He had a job to do - the due processes of the law - what had that got to do with nerves?

First of all they tell you which side the heart is. So that you can imagine it there - almost. Say you imagined your heart was in your left boot. Then when you got a sore foot you could say you had a heart attack. that might kill you that might. Especially if you believed it was fatal. Some did. White man's magic my friend. Stick to weights. They were bloody heavy. They said the body had natural laws. That didn't seem right to him. It was a matter of self-control. Imposed like. Authority. You couldn't let your body run wild so to speak. If that's what they meant by laws of nature. Oh no. Forever watchful. Watch it. Watch it. You can't tell me that a law of nature is an excuse for that sort of behaviour. There was only one sort of law in Hedge's book – man-made and imposed with due reverence, etc, etc...

Nevertheless he would have a checkup. Just a checkup. No nonsense. A little on the side. not enough to compromise himself.

CHAPTER VI

He sat on a log and surveyed the British vegetation. British bees were buzzing round British flowers, how reassuring. God was an Englishman in all but name, the same manners. Lord. We had English lords and the Lord God so He was in with the same crowd. Comrade God was more in the line of Jesus. It was class. It depended which class you belonged to. Which class you were born into. Jesus was born in a stable so it took a tremendous effort to overcome that disadvantage and fair do's he had done it...

A policeman's lot is a lonely lot. They don't understand these criminals - all this civilian mob too - all the rubbish out there - how would they know what goes on in a copper's mind? It's alright if you get on with the chaps - a lot goes on in uniform that is is not generally recognised. Not that he would call himself unpopular. What did they think of him? All the people in the Force should be for each other. But jealousy was rife. Rife. He was fairly certain the Super liked him. Now that could help in a tight corner but say you got a gun against your ribs and you think that back at the Station they're all laughing at you? I mean you feel like turning it in - you do - I mean he was doing his job just to impress the chaps - he wanted them to accept him. He had been on lots of cases some of them high profile but somehow that magic seemed to elude him - popularity. The opposite was happening. To hell with 'em...

He had a job to do.

They gave you pills for nerves. The very thought made him nervy. The body made its own chemical compounds didn't it? It was like a pharmacy - like your own body was a drugs company manufacturing whatever you needed but the management was out of control according to the doctors - gone wild - so they stepped in and took control the doctors did - with their pills - their medicines - and all around us were plants. But which ones one would do the inspector good? He gazed at the vegetation in wonder...

Now my boy don't let the bastards get you down - that's the secret of success - indifference! We've all got a living to earn - but not by interfering with people...

It was not natural - there was the bug - this bug code name Green Swan - well I suppose if they're ill and dying off like flies there must be a   bug - you had to believe in something - if you couldn't believe in God anymore at least you could believe in a bug - though you couldn't see either - never mind their microscopes - they can always show you something and call it a bug that was his attitude - though to be fair that was as far as this case went - not the wonders of science which he was determined must not dazzle him. Because he was dealing with the downside - the dark side - someone had created a bug and called it the Green Swan. This was an unknowable area until he brought all his training into focus on this case - his case - his next case - coming up any moment any time - with their ingratiating smiles and condescending professional secrecy that he would break through like the undergrowth that contained still yes - magical plants that could make him well. If he needed them...

He had to face that fear was part of a policeman's lot. Though he had his inflatable policewoman and was not completely alone. But he couldn't be with blowing her up all the time. He had to learn to face things with her deflated. Depressed even. That's the way it had to be. Tough. It meant he could operate quicker. After all if he was forever blowing her up every time he panicked he'd never get his man. He'd get away...

Also with her inflated he was vulnerable. For they might turn on her so to speak. Why had he brought her along with him? She was his partner that's why. They were professionals. A team. What went on between them was their business. An affair. It was their secret. The Met had come up with the scheme - OK get on with it - no argument. An economy drive. Doris, his inflatable policewoman, had no salary and no pension rights. It was a stone bonker saving for them. The accountants. They had to balance the books - the Bigwigs - to please their Higher Ups. But they weren't at the sharp end were they? That's where he worked. Lived and breathed. He was in the field. With her. Doris. They would make the best of it. See it through. Get a result. Just Do It...

I'm a loner, thought Hedge. That's the way I like it. He was tempted to throw away his bicycle pump. To do without Doris. To have no means of inflating her. But that wasn't the attitude. And the pump was official property. And after all in a crisis...

I mustn't turn to her in a crisis, he thought. More for sympathy and rest. That was not in the manual on usage of an inflatable partner. The inflatable guide to policewomen. He blew up his manual and consulted the rubber. In ridged words it instructed only, AVOID PUNCTURE BY GUNFIRE. Or did it? Or was it? What?

For her. For Doris. And for himself. Not to be punctured by gunfire seemed a good idea.

Could this Bug - assume bug - viral condition - be the disastrous outcome of a germ warfare project? The thought hit Inspector Hedge like a rocket missile. Could - hold it - yes - come on follow the rabbit down the hole into this wonderland of government subterfuge - could the incurables be infected scientists? Mark Possible. Green Swan outcome...

He was glad he had not brought his pet dog from the police kennels. These poor Alsatians had not been taught to attack scientists - only criminals - little did they, the dogs, know of the fears of vivisection. If they were going to send our dogs out into cases like this - nursing homes and all - they should be trained to smell a scientist a mile off. He would mention it to the Super upon his return. Assume return. He might get a mention in the Police Dog Training Manual. How fleeting is fame, he sighed. Let the labour be it's own reward...

The truth was the the Inspector's briefing was nebulous. A banana for breakfast was all very well but it was not much to go on. He liked to arrive and make a bit of a splash with an immediate arrest having worked the whole thing out on his way to the scene of the crime. True you might get the wrong man but by saving time you could often make the case stick. He wondered was there really any such thing as the wrong man? Brothers under the skin. Often he had hidden in his wardrobe when a murder had been reported. How well he knew they could get the wrong man. The chickens could come home to roost. It was an act of boldness which made him leap from the wardrobe into the room and grab his uniform and don it assuming the full majesty of the law. You were safer in a uniform, believe me...

Methinks he doth protest too much. Hedge often wondered whether the Super was after him to pin a string of unsolved sex murders on him. After all it would be a brilliant stroke to work from inside the Force these nefarious crimes. Maybe he should resign to avoid suspicion. But it was too late for that and would only draw more attention upon himself. If he had not joined he could have taken his chance like any ordinary civilian. Who knows what his Superintendent was cooking up to put a feather in his own cap - what hapless victim he had in mind - and even possibly - possibly - the Super could be the serial sex killer. That would add up. Promotion was the spur, that was for sure. To perpetrate a crime and to solve it by shopping someone else? That was something to get up for in the morning.

He knew he had not murdered anyone. It was so unfair. The strain. Anyway he could not be blamed for this incurable murder. He was curable.

CHAPTER VII

Doctor Fettle was furious with the roses this year. He roamed the nursing home grounds silently ranting and raving. The petals were falling off and making a mess. No sooner had they blossomed this year than there was a mess to clear up. The trees were as bad but they would not shed their leaves until autumn and they could wait. He would rake up the leaves and burn them. He quite liked this task, the seasonal smell of the bonfire. But picking up these errant rose petals one by one (with a pair of tweezers) well what could you do with them? Stick them back on? Eat them? To tell the truth nature pained the virile doctor. Human beings were so much easier to keep clean and tidy than plant life. More amenable to discipline. Though all his hedges and bushes were a topiary lesson. He insisted on military cuts on a fortnightly basis.

Fettle had been an army doctor. Frontline stuff. They had been trained to treat trauma battle wounds on dogs. Or pigs. You shot them, tended the poor wounded creatures back to relative health and then destroyed them. That was the final exercise before qualification. With Fettle it had taken three dogs. Though he was not required to do it he had shot the first two himself, too close to the heart and they died on him before he could get them onto the operating table. This was a pity because he wanted to see the whole process through himself. The third dog someone else, more practised in the art, shot and wounded. He treated the animal rather successfully - it was in his report - and then destroyed it by lethal injection. After that he was ready for anything. Anything the army could serve up.

In the front line, briefly, he had been tempted to shoot his own men and then to treat them back to an assurance of survival and - who knows - perhaps later to administer a lethal injection. But he had toed the line. Perhaps he had over-trained for the job. True, a war zone was no time or place for sentiment. Thus he had come to to be appointed to this post where the anaesthetising of his feelings had been taken into account. He could be counted on to do whatever. Later, later...

Inspector Hedge burst through the rose bushes covered in blossom.

Are you drunk? demanded Doctor Fettle.

Never drink on duty, answered Hedge quickly.

My dear chap, said the doctor. Could it possibly be that you are the man we've been waiting for? The one they promised to send?

The one and only Inspector Hedge. My card.

The inspector produced a card and handed it to the doctor.

But my dear fellow, said the doctor, this card is intensely black.

Yes, I am in mourning for my life, said Hedge. It is a personal matter and does not need to come between me and my duties.

I shall bear that in mind, said the doctor.

Hedge laughed. You get it? He said.

I get it, said the doctor. Yes, that's a good one.

Nevertheless...

A tall thin man standing in a bathchair - bolt upright standing to attention, passed them by pushed by a male nurse.

It's amazing how he keeps his balance, quipped Fettle.

Is that one of your incurables? Asked Hedge.

Oh no, said Fettle, we keep our incurables forty feet under ground in a concrete bunker ward.

Well when do we start digging, said Hedge. I must see them soon.

But there was a twinkle in his eye and Fettle saw that he was not meant to take him seriously. They both laughed. Fettle, calculating, was the first to stop.

There is another way in, he said.

One up to you, thought Hedge. Tread carefully with this man.

Did you come alone? asked Doctor Fettle.

No, I have a van full of police dogs back on the road, answered Hedge.

Interesting, Fettle parried.

I should warn you, said Hedge. If you've any thoughts of vivisection they have been trained against it. One sign of a needle and they'll be at your throat. And the same goes for me too, my friend. I have not come here to finish up on your operating table.

Oh come now, the doctor replied, rolling his eyes to reassure his visitor. We do have a waiting list you know.

The thin tall gentleman standing in the bath chair was pushed back behind them by the muscled male nurse.

Leave yourself alone Mr Plerns! Shouted Doctor Fettle.

A faint moan escaped the lips of Mr Plerns.

Some of them are at it all the time, explained the doctor.

That is none of my business, replied Inspector Hedge.

They retard from a hostile environment into fantasies, as do most people from time to time. The doctor stared at Hedge.

In a lesser way, said Hedge.

Of course. Not clinically. The trauma leads them to a favourite fantasy endlessly elaborated where they seek and find release.

The inspector was breathing more heavily. I can only repeat that is none of my business, he said. I have a job to do and I quote... I have a job to do. Tell me, Doctor, do you only have incurables in this nursing home?

I've already answered that, replied Fettle sharply. The contaminated ones are forty foot under.

He prodded into the earth with his pruning fork.

When they die they might be able come up a few feet. It's an unusual direction for the dead to take, what?

If contaminated surely a cremation is in order? Hedge replied.

Of course, Inspector. Please forgive my flippancy. Such is the strain here humour is the only thing that keeps us sane. Relatively that is.

I can relate to that in my own professional capacity, said Hedge. I'm up for a laugh as you might have noticed?

Glint of steel beneath that...

Well...

The doctor took the inspector in with a friendly smile. I can take it. Gallows humour gets us through in this job. So shoot.

Right. Without messing around I must insist that you give me all the information I require.

Impossible, said Fettle. Official Secrets Act.

Which part of the Act is that?

The sexual part, ha ha. Have you not heard of the Sexual Act? Recently passed by Parliament. It's got lots of little clauses...

And I've got lots of little toes's, said Hedge. But I can't muck around here all afternoon. Your wit is losing me, frankly. So, my good chap, kindly escort me to the ward...

CHAPTER VIII

In the lift was a small desk.

Choose your floor, said the doctor gaily, as he sat behind the desk.

Now let's have a few details shall we?

What floor? said the inspector doggedly.

Take your pick, we can stop anywhere.

I'm afraid, said the inspector, that it is me – I – who require the information. About which floor - to start with - and no prevarication if you please.

Then you don't want a quick check-up?

The inspector's eyes narrowed.

Only you seem to have a bit of a flush old chap.

That's none of your business – I've been sent on a case, not for a health check.

Rotten luck! Anyway you've come to the right place if you do feel a bit under the weather – I could take your pulse?

That's where it starts, isn't it? One thing leads to another. It'll be an

X-ray next. I have an entirely different concept. I see myself as a child of nature.

But nature is sickening so what of the child, said the doctor.

The lift stopped at the third floor – down.

Minus three, quoth the doctor. The incurables are minus four – after that there's only the basement.

What do you keep in that?

Coal.

Isn't this a smokeless zone?

Their conversation was getting nowhere. Minus four arrived.

Shall we get out? Asked the doctor.

Not yet, said Hedge. Hang on. I've got lots of time.

You need not worry. The whole level is not contagious. Everything is contained.

I would assume so, doctor.

Why do you carry those weights everywhere?

I was 'weighting' for you to ask me that. A foolish pun...

One not resisted...

Forgive me. We in the force believe in perfect fitness - with the fitness of the body...

And a smart tunic, Officer...

Comes the fitness of the mind.

Many an ill man has been a genius, said Fettle. Health is not everything. In fact I would say that it's over-rated. When it gets to the point of phobia. A fear of what? Warding off the unknown. It can only go on so long.

My point. My point, said Hedge.

The lift started ascending again.

These weights are mighty heavy, said Hedge, I take them everywhere I go.

What even swimming?

Underwater.

It would have to be.

You've heard of the strong arm of the law? Take a gander at these. Inspector Hedge whipped off his jacket and tautened his left bicep.

You can relax now, said the doctor.

Thank you. The inspector replaced his jacket.

You have a healthy frame there – not much to worry about, said Fettle;

Taa, said Hedge. Not that I'm taking your word for it.

As you please.

The lift rang ground floor.

Are we going down again? Asked Fettle.

To the incurables, yes. Come on.

The lift descended and once more arrived at minus four. The doors drew open and they alighted.

They were greeted by a man in a green smock.

This is Sir Hilary Spong – the severe ear, eyes, nose, throat, knees and bumps-a- daisy specialist, introduced Doctor Fettle.

How do you do, said Sir Hilary Spong, I'm also in attendance to the Queen.

You're a bit late today, said Hedge, keeping his humour up to the mark as he worked through this trickiest of tricky cases.

Have you seen them yet? said Fettle taking Hilary (Sir) to one side. Hedge tried to overhear. But made it conspicuous by tying up his boot lace. He contrived to tie them together by some misfortune and fell flat on his face as they called him over.

You might as well be in on this, said Fettle. In case there's anything vital - for your case what?

I've been studying their reward system, said Sir Hilary. Looking for signs of weakness. Fletcher - he picks his nose - now if we could stop him

- then he would want to gratify himself some other way - for instance he might take to chocolate - chocolate pudding - which we would control.

Yes, Sir Ralph.

Sir Hilary, corrected Sir Hilary.

Sorry. Yes, very well we stop him picking his nose but he might start picking his feet - self-gratification wise - difficult case - we've got to get him out more - wanting more - more of what we can supply...

You could always try strawberry whip, said Sir Hilary. He put his stethoscope away.

Handy little thing, he remarked. Remarkably good for conversations when you don't want to hear what the other chap's saying - always use it at the club what.

I'll say.

The medical profession had finished their conversation, and Hedge moved closer. He was done with diversions.

Where are the incurables? demanded the inspector bluntly. Time to front up, gentlemen.

Fettle went to the wall of the white corridor and pressed a button. A strange machine turned out from the wall – small and compact.

What's that for? demanded Hedge.

Making milkshakes. OK fun's over. You asked for it, Inspector.

Fettle was obviously rattled. Now which blasted button is it? He pressed the green button and a steel shutter slid up revealing an obser-vation window. Through the window could be seen the ward. Incurable. Four inmates.

My word, said Hedge, just like the real thing. All that lot in there -incurable are they - well let's have a look at 'em - work to do.

Hedge went towards what appeared to be a door.

No! Shouted Doctor Fettle. Then gentler. But no old chap - you can't go in there - the bug.

The Bug?

The bug, repeated Fettle reverently. It - beg pardon - the bug is highly contagious - no-one can enter that ward - sorry - sorry pal.

Hedge didn't like being called pal, but left it for the time being.

How on earth am I going to investigate the case?

Hardly worth it, Fettle nodded.

What are you nodding for?

I'm nodding in agreement with myself, said Fettle.

Here I'll – I'll do that for you, said Sir Hilary, and started nodding in agreement.

You don't have to do that Sir Hilary.

Nonsense - carry on...

How could Hedge break through this double act? He wasn't about to play the musical saw or do bird impressions. He waited it out.

Doctor Fettle continued, OK this is it. Surely they told you at the Yard that all these poor devils will be dead within two weeks? What price justice old chap – highly contagious the lot – can't move 'em out – how are you going to administer to them? Whatever it is you're bringing. Why even the vicar sends the holy communion through the post.

Who takes the post in? Hedge was quick.

The vicar – got guts – say that much for him.

Well if he delivers the post in he doesn't need to send the Holy Communion by Royal Mail.

The. vicar goes in there most times. Me, I'm terrified to catch the bug – my dear chap its curtains – why should I risk my life? I can't do anything for them if I become sick as well – let 'em rot.

Sir Hilary was still nodding.

Surely you don't agree Sir Hilary? Hedge enquired.

Errr no – what – what do you mean?

You were nodding, sir...

Well cancel those last few nods. He turned to Doctor Fettle. After all doctor we must sometimes take a risk ourselves for the sake of medicine.

I don't really see why sir, said Fettle bluntly. Or how you applying your stethoscope to the window while they press their chest the other side...

Enough, interrupted Sir Hilary. I have my methods. It's to do with morale of the patient.

He stepped into the lift. I expect we'll be seeing quite a lot of each other, Inspector, said Sir Hilary.

Well as a medical specialist you may see more of me, said Hedge. Deep breath, hold it and cough.

That's a good line and I would suggest you seek help.

Of what sort?

Of the sort that could keep you alive in a place like this, suggested Sir Hilary softly.

I think we understand each other, sir.

I hardly understand myself, said the specialist. So let us not presume too much. Then louder, Goodbye for now! And the lift was gone.

Hedge turned to Doctor Fettle who was waving at the incurable patients through the window. Had he heard that little exchange with Sir Hilary? He gave no indication of it and addressed his patients,

Good morning, you little miseries! He grinned at them, mouthing words they could not hear. Come on wave back you little buggers - be shot of all of you in a couple of weeks - get on with some preventive medicine then. Something useful when this farce is played out.

No-one can be seen to be beyond the reach of law, said the inspector. He stared through the observation window. One of the patients waved at him - showing a brief interest in a rare visitor - then returned to his jigsaw puzzle. For the others what can be said? Nothing out of the ordinary. Pick your murderer. Why would anybody bother? It was so pointless.

CHAPTER IX

Come this way Inspector.

Hedge found himself in a laboratory. It was quite large and a white coated figure wearing a modern gas-mask passed down the end carrying a cage of rats.

Belcher! shouted Fettle.

Belcher startled dropped the cage which broke open and the rats scurried out and ran in all directions.

You fool Belcher! That's most unhygienic!

Belcher grabbed a spray gun and chased the rats. Hedge jumped out onto a stool, sweating.

Several of the rats were caught with the spray and died instantly. The others disappeared.

The rats had been injected sir - the half-hour serum - they would be dead anyway soon.

You're an idiot Belcher - how can we cut 'em up if we're searching under benches and - oh for their little corpses...

Can't we talk elsewhere? Asked Hedge clambering down from the stool.

Certainly, come into my office.

In the office Hedge collapsed into a chair.

Don't you like rats? enquired Fettle.

By all means - experiment on the vermin - kill them - kill them - beastly horrible - operate - just leave our dogs alone - rats - they've got it coming.

So you're not against vivisection?

I hate rats.

What do you feel about elephants?

A panel, indeed the whole wall, turned opaque and then cloudy, cleared, a sort of glass. Through it Hedge saw a field and in it three lovely elephants.

You don't experiment on them? Demanded Hedge.

We're having trouble getting them in the laboratory.

But they're beautiful, said Hedge, I'd love to ride on one.

Oh have done with such childish things, said Fettle. It's a grotesque world and we're trying to cope. The elephants must take their chance like the rest of us.

A baby elephant swayed up near the glass window.

Where'd you pinch these? Get 'em from a zoo did you?

Top secret - but my dear Inspector you've come here on a case not on behalf of the antivivisection league.

I'll - I'll tell my Super about these elephants – look here what are you going to do to them?

First we must build the appropriate chambers for them - do you know Inspector off the record - Great Britain is the first civilised country in the world to experiment with elephants.

Doctor Fettle prepared a needle, Now just roll up your sleeve please. Hedge jolted back Oh no what's that?

Fettle pressed a button and the wall returned - a sort of illusion of wallpaper.

My dear Inspector - I would like to inject you against possible contamination by the bug.

Does it work?

Do you wish to enter that ward Inspector?

I'm determined to Doctor - determined - it's my job.

Then roll up your sleeve.

But...

Hedge rolled up his sleeve and winced as the needle went home.

Fettle smiled. There.

Look - what have you done to me - what are you smiling at?

Fettle wiped the small wound with cotton wool, and Hedge rolled his sleeve down. They had told him nothing about this at the Yard. He hated injections. He felt invaded. What had happened to his one and indivisible body. He fainted.

CHAPTER X

When Hedge came to he was in a private ward. Had he seen the elephants? Such was his first thought. Belcher came in and grabbed his pulse. Hedge pulled his arm away.

Hold on that's my pulse - leave it alone - what's going on?

We are cheeky this morning aren't we?

What morning?

Belcher reached out and firmly took the inspector's pulse.

Where are my clothes - now look here my boy it will pay you to co-operate with me - I never forget a face...

You've never seen such goings on as 'ere, said Belcher mysteriously. Oh my, Inspector, your pulse is really rhythmic isn't it?

I'm glad you noticed. We could be in the Hammersmith Palais doing the rhumba!

Shall we dance? Said Belcher and took out a thermometer.

Oh no, said Hedge, not that thank you. I've had enough of this case - where are my clothes - and things - my weights and all that...?

He longed for his inflatable policewoman. For here surely was an emergency. There was safety in numbers. In his shoulder bag was bicycle pump one, banana skin empty, inflatable darling one. He had said darling. No - he had thought darling. The thought precedes the act. Things were going a bit far. And there was that brute trying to take his temperature.

I want my bag, said Hedge.

Well I'll go and look for it if you'll let me take your temperature - come on love - let's be having you.

And she thrust the thermometer into his mouth. She had a big bunch of keys she did - which SHE jangled on a chain - and sang softly,

In Dublin's fair city,

Where the boys are so pretty,

I first set my eyes on sweet Michael Malone...

Go on you great big Nellie, thought, Hedge. I've met your type at the police ball. Surprising when they let their hair down some of 'em but then are we so different?

Darling. The word stuck in his throat. With the thermometer. Had he really thought darling one, about the inflatable. Just a piece of rubber. Things were going to pieces. And those elephants were giving him a hell of a worrying concern. He'd like to save them. It wasn't his job. It wasn't fair. Elephants.

Above normal, said Belcher shaking the thermometer down again.

It's always above normal - me and Trotsky - funny - we both had temperatures.

Don't bring politics into this ward dear.

No - I mean we were both a degree over - where are my clothes - my plain clothes?

They looked rather fancy to me love - I don't think you should call them plain - you don't do yourself a favour.

Hedge was lost without his clothes. How could he administer the law? He had on a pair of ill-fitting pyjamas which he noticed with alarm as he tried to get out of bed. He wobbled and sat back on the bed.

That injection knocked you back a bit dear - take it easy do.

That injection - that inj - blast - his mind was wandering. What with the elephants. He would rather save them. But how to contact the zoo keeper. The Super. The Super of the zoo. The Yard was a zoo. The smells sometimes made him sick. They behaved like animals. He'd seen it. And they didn't like him. The Super. Could he be contacted. Belcher tucked him back into bed.

I wish to contact the Superintendent of the London Zoo - it's urgent.

Take it easy dear - you're really not well enough for day trips yet.

Where's the doctor - I've had enough - I want my clothes.

Toodlepip! And the male nurse Belcher went out jangling her keys.

Hedge thought, Oh dear how come I'm compromised? Already. In over my head. An inpatient. In pyjamas. This is rubbish. How can I turn it to my advantage? Am I perceiving it correctly or am I already the victim of...? Have they got inside my head? How would I know?

He dozed off and when he woke again he could not tell what time of the night or day it was. Electric light overhead. Was that a window? He longed for a view of the elephants. It was a window painted onto the wall with a view of a shunting yard. That really wasn't good enough. They could have painted elephants. He got out of bed and stood up. Firm. Yes. Walked a pace and didn't stagger. That's better. Out into the corridor. The white ambulance man hadn't locked the door. He'd get the bitch for that - report her - negligence - though to be fair it could be deliberate. Policy as ordained from on high. Leave the door open. They had the upper hand - they were playing games with him weren't they? Well he could play a losing hand until it was time to upset the cards grab a table leg and bash their heads in - I mean you didn't mess around on a job like this.

Meanwhile he was out in the white tube. Minus four? He couldn't tell what minus level he was on.

45

And then it struck him.

How could he see elephants on a minus four level?

Perhaps it was an underground field. There was no limit to what these germ-warfare scientists would get up to for already a theory was developing in Hedge's head.

Inspector Hedge saw the lift and climbed in. Yes it registered minus four. Where to go now? He'd try minus two - and pressed the button. He went through the drawers of the doctors desk in the lift. They were all empty except in one - where he met a big spider sitting on an envelope. He started back, whipped off his shoe and hammered the spider. Finally picked it up. It was of course made of rubber and precious time had been lost. He grabbed the envelope as the lift clocked minus two and chimed twice.

Inspector Hedge in his large pyjamas stepped out of the lift at minus two level onto a spring board high above a pool. Before he knew it he was at the end and saw for a moment the admiring faces below. He stumbled and tried to dive. The most awful belly flop. Three was scored on the cards by the judges. Fettle reached out a hand to help the inspector from the pool.

Well done - I didn't know you were entering - very therapeutic - good for mind and body - my dear fellow - you needed a costume.

Never mind that, said Hedge recovering his composure. That's a silly thing to have outside a lift.

My dear chap - some of our competitors are invalids.

The lift doors opened once more and a man with a crutch hobbled out and fell off the board - his crutch flew away from him - as he hit the water his heavily bandaged foot was the first to surface. The judges signalled a two. A wheel chair was brought to the edge of the pool as the wet patient was hauled out and his stick rescued with him. Male nurse

Belcher pushed the wretched shaking wet mass of patient in the wheel-chair along the pool's edge and hurried him out through the swing door marked Changing Rooms. Other patients listlessly watched the proceedings. An underwater swimming pool. Whatever next.

I suppose it's not surprising, commented Hedge. After all two floors down below is an underground park with elephants.

My dear chap you'll catch a fever all wet - elephants nonsense.

You showed them to me doctor.

You're shivering - hallucinations old chap - the anti-serum treatment sometimes produces them.

I saw elephants first I tell you before you injected me.

Time factor loss old chap - what a muddle - come on - let's get your clothes on.

Clothes! But... Inspector Hedge dribbled on as he was led from the pool, there was - that is - the poor brutes - vivisection of elephants whatever...

Whatever next, quipped Fettle merrily. Some job for the surgeons, eh? They could get lost inside an elephant - excavation work - what a challenge - come on old chap...

Hedge found his clothes in the cubicle. No weights. No satchel. The doctor lent him coins for a hair cream squirt. After the dryer that was, great fun with a foot pedal operation and free. Hedge had to laugh. For a brisk rub down with a fresh towel marked "Howling Nursing Home" had restored his sense of balance. Orientation in his body, natural well-being. Fettle coaxed him to weigh himself, producing another coin.

Forever in your debt, said Hedge stepping onto the scales. Quite slim. Just over his boyish weight. A hell of a regime. No sweeties from the police canteen like some of the pigs. Pigs. Great fat coppers with fat bottoms. Thank God some in the force kept a sense of proportion. He was not going to any suburb to rot away - fourteen stone of law and order. Oh no.

God you've got a boyish figure for a man of your age, said the doctor. Plenty of swimming, said Hedge, I'd like another go - I could improve my score - where do I get in the lift? But it was silly for he had dried off dressed and slick combed his hair smart-like and he had a job to do. Feeling good had it's problems too, he must not get careless. He was still not sure about the elephants but thank God the effects of the needle had worn off. He would keep his conclusions suspicions etc. to himself for the meanwhile. Perhaps Sir Hilary was an agent on his side. Perhaps not. Anyway what next?

Fettle gathered up his wet pyjamas. Hedge snatched the wringing garments away.

I'll do the dirty work, said Hedge.

I was going to let Belcher our white powered National Front nursy take them to the drying room.

Belcher appeared. Bathing costume flippers and snorkel mask. Fettle beckoned for him to remove the mask.

You don't need a mask on outside the lab Belcher.

Belcher raised the snorkel off his face. This one would not be useful in the lab, Doctor, however short we are of equipment. I would not venture into the incurable ward like this. Or Yours Truly would be a goner.

You are familiar with Inspector Hedge I take it.

Not so you'd notice, dear.

You must cooperate with him Nurse.

What, with a patient? Or has he come to spoil the party? We were happy on our own without him weren't we? All of life was ours to observe - through the window so to speak. So what's he want? He can't change anything.

There's such a thing as law and order, growled Hedge.

And chaos. And beauty. And change, said Belcher. You cling on as best you can now, darling. This is the last frontier this is. You've stepped beyond the things you know so watch it. His expression clouded with a sullen hatred.

He's the one I'll have to watch, thought the inspector.

The moment passed as Belcher's face cleared. He jangled his keys - his prissy self again - toying with them coyly on a chain.

Last one in's a sissy, he cried out as he pulled down the snorkel mask and flip flopped off down the poolside to the deep end. He stepped off the edge and sank like a stone into the green antiseptic water.

Don't make the blasted keys rusty, yelled Fettle after him. Too late.

While Doctor Fettle's mind was diverted, Hedge slipped the soggy envelope into his own dry clothes then handed the pyjamas to the doctor with a twisted smile. That should fool him.

I must see the incurables, said Hedge, I shouldn't imagine they'd be allowed in the water.

If they left the ward we'd shoot 'em, said Fettle. Sirens, robot dogs, full evacuation procedures God what a tragedy that would be. No-one would be safe. The district would be devastated. Cancel the annual flower show.

Even if injected, asked Hedge.

I took a chance giving you that, said Fettle. Listen, we are self contained here - we have to be - makes for insularity so please forgive any odd behaviour amongst the staff. He led the inspector to a cafeteria and bought two teas.

Hedge wondered who had taken the chance. Was he a guinea pig being given a trial vaccine? When a spare body strayed into their orbit it was of use to medical science alive or dead at Howlings Nursing Home. Apparently. But what was apparent and what was hard fact? He'd have his work cut out deciding that. And... Get this! He was aware that the instrument at work - his own mind that is - was not objective but subjective no amount of training could remove that. He was one up on his comrades in blue there who could never get beyond the next prejudice reinforced by jokes in the bar. No matter how many courses they went on...

Fettle led him up some steps to the pool gallery where they sat. Hedge viewed the pool. There. Agony. Rage. There was that rat Belcher sporting in the water with his inflatable policewoman. Hedge found a whistle in his pocket and blew.

That man - that man there - shouted Hedge. He was on the spot. For he could not admit she was a policewoman inflatable. He needed at least one anonymous ally.

What, said Fettle, come now Belcher - no swimming aids.

Fettled nudged Hedge to follow him. Work, said the Doctor.

Hedge faced an agonising decision. He had not given the game away.

And for now had to leave her. With that white flowered pock-marked lily. They left the pool - medicine and law.

CHAPTER XI

Friday. A charter plane apparently flying to Borneo disappeared over the Indian Ocean. The bodies of five scientists who it was reported were on their way to a germ-warfare disarmament conference – control and non-proliferation - were lost in the shark-infested waters. Great Britain mourned the loss of these important men. Why Borneo? One might be tempted to ask and risk a five o'clock in the morning knock on the door for having had the temerity to ask.

CHAPTER XII

Meanwhile dear Inspector Hedge - to himself inconsolable but he knew not why - why he was grieving - was it truly for his own life that he mourned - anyway he continued his relentless investigation of the incurables. Oh my self-doubting, self-loathing, self-judging and yet to be self-loving and forgiving Inspector Hedge! He was his job. Which was a dangerous precedent he had set himself. Never mind. He had a murder to solve. They were in the morgue and Fettle continued to instruct,

The big problem Inspector is the decontamination of the bodies.

How many people have died of the bug so far?

None yet - just our little catastrophe.

The murder - but how can you be so sure they'll all be dead within a fortnight?

Ahh Doubting Thomas - you cannot question everything in this world my dear Inspector - you have to take some things on trust.

They were standing by a machine that hummed. Inside viewed through perspex lay the corpse of Ernie.

I suppose you will return the body to the relatives sooner or later?

Out of the question, replied Fettle, strictly D List.

Beg pardon.

That body is restricted information - it's more or less Government property - our Ernie is still on salary you know - more use to us dead than alive - I can't tell you any more at this stage….

I notice some scratch marks round the throat - would you in your capacity as doctor…

Thank you.

… say that this was related to the cause of death?

Doctor Fettle laughed. My dear chap - those scratches could be marks of passion - love or violence - love and violence - yes our Ernie may well have been a victim of a crime passionnel.

Please speak English, said Hedge, taking notes.

You've got an interesting shaped head, said Doctor Fettle thought-fully.

Hedge touched his head. And ran his fingers through his hair. Better make a note of it. He wondered should he spring his theory on the doctor. An element of surprise. It was obvious to Hedge. This was a germ-warfare case. A mistaken experiment. An exploding test tube. And the lot cop it. Cover it up. Oh yes. None of his business. The murder was his business. And yet he was on the brink of a bigger crime. Official. Official Secrets Act.

Fettle turned and tuned up the machine while he spoke. Thoughts are running through your head Inspector Hedge - that are none of your busi-ness - you have a murder to solve - stick to that.

How will I get my man out of here?

Impossible! Futile - we can't contaminate the Old Bailey can we? Anyway my dear chap by the time the wheels of justice have been put into operation they'll all be dead - the murderer an' all - so speaking of justice rough justice will have been done.

Life is cheap in the incurable ward.

Who said that? Hedge turned and standing behind him was the rat Belcher.

Is everything ready for the ship's concert tonight? enquired Fettle.

Yes sir, simpered Belcher, I'll be wearing my best drag.

That's my girl, said Fettle, I say Inspector you might like to come along and meet a few of the passengers.

Inspector Hedge decided to play along with this one. Information was what he required.

Certainly, he answered, Is it on B Deck?

They all laughed. Would Belcher bring the inflatable policewoman along? Hedge daren't ask. Ship. What ship? Hardship mate! Play along with them for the time being...

CHAPTER XIII

If you knew Suzy like I knew Suzy! Belcher was giving it strong on the mike. He looked delightful in the cheekiest mini of all things and a lovely lace blouse like. Even Hedges head was turned. They were in the pool. Decked out gloriously. There were rubber dinghies floating about with various patients aboard. Fettle on a large platform mid-pool entertained his guests - in his captain's uniform he cut a fine figure. There were fairy lights everywhere and a real festive atmosphere ensued. Though the patients didn't look very excited, Mr Plerns was afloat on his wheel-chair which had two rubber cylinders strapped under it. Plerns still stood rigidly to attention in a dinky sailor suit this time – quite appropriate to the occasion as he drifted past. There was a little flag - an ensign which fluttered gaily from the back of the wheel-chair. Hedge was at the Captain's table eating soup as the platform rocked slightly. He felt a bit sick. Where was She? The inflatable one. He hadn't seen her yet.

Captain Fettle leaned across.

Hello there - enjoying the trip?

Aye Aye, said Hedge dourly.

He was not dressed up. He hadn't brought anything exciting to wear, not expecting anything like this. Down at the end of the pool from the table buffet waiters loaded a dinghy with the main course and set out paddling towards the platform. There was a great to do as they arrived, but all was managed very well with the mooring rope tied to Hedge's leg. He did not complain. Information was what he required.

Doctor Fettle had refused to take him into the incurable ward. Yet. There was a take factor with the injection. And Fettle could clear him in the morning. If the positive factor had operated - bug wise. It was all double dutch to Hedge but he had to co-operate - to some extent. Meanwhile he had been given a pretty room. Really it was a private ward. He had wanted to protest. He was not a patient. But it was a bed. It was the same room as he had come to in after the injection but they had changed the curtains. It was still a bit too medical for Hedge's liking for the pattern on the curtains was hypodermics and kidney bowls. However, be that as it may, he was in full employment. None but the brave...

Belcher was swinging now with a new number as he sidled round the mike stroking it and all that. Wish he'd fall in the water thought Hedge. Belcher did have an attractive voice though.

Mirror mirror on the wall...
Who's the fairest of them all...
Your mommas good looking...
And your Daddy's ten foot tall...

The lights went out. They heard the lift door slide open. There was a small explosion and a parachute flare illuminated the pool. The vicar was standing on the springboard. He intoned "For what you are about to receive may the Lord make you truly grateful, Amen."

We're half-way through the nosh up already Vicar! Shouted Captain Fettle jovially.

Oh in that case carry on, called out the vicar. Sorry I'm late everyone! Getting to know you! He did a beautiful header into the pool.

A spot played upon Hedge and everybody burst into Happy Birthday to you - Happy Birthday to you – Happy Birthday dear Inspector Hedge - Happy Birthday to you…

So it is, thought Hedge. How the hell did they know? Of course medical details, date of birth. The spot went out as Fettle leant across and touched his arm. Watch this. A cake with forty-two candles burst to the surface of the water.

Clever little trick what? said Fettle. Would you care to say a few words?

My teeth were never in a glass, said Hedge. I always keep them in in company.

A frogman surfaced beside the cake and pushed it to the platform edge. The lights came on again.

Got a little note from the Super, said Fettle. Best wishes. You are never out of his thoughts - he thinks a lot of you.

So Doctor Fettle was in contact with the Yard. The pigs. The golden trough. Information. At last. Hedge heard the vague trumpeting of an elephant. He stared at Fettle who showed no signs of having heard that exotic jungle call. You see, he was saying, I reported the murder naturally to the Yard. Your Superman I suppose. There's no big mystery here my dear Jack...

He knows my name as well. Oh we are all familiar! This case was hard enough to crack. They seemed to know more about him than he knew about them. Join in the fun though. Someone will let slip something...

The vicar joined the party on the platform as Hedge cut the cake. Again - slightly louder - that trumpeting. It must be an elephant. Where was Tarzan?

Happy birthday, said the vicar, who was wearing a long plastic cassock that shed the water easily. We haven't met. You must come to our little chapel in the grounds - sometime we have little religious happenings - done away with the old services - we've got the Ku Klux Klan in next week - they're doing a foreign tour.

While the vicar chattered it did not go unnoticed to Hedge that Fettle had nodded to the blossoming Belcher who picked up his handbag and left the pool area. Hedge was sure it was something to do with the elephant sound.

You know, said the vicar, life does get a bit tedious here - I'm glad of the incurables in a way - I had to pluck up my courage - hate the needle - but I got a positive - and as long as they don't bite you...

Who?

The incurables - they get bitter sometimes.

Are they religious vicar?

Don't know - doesn't do to talk about religion - too controversial - sex religion and politics I steer clear of the lot - everyone's entitled to their own opinion.

Well you have a Sunday service don't you?

Don't work Sundays old chap - five day week - it's fair...

Again that elephant trumpeting.

Can you hear an elephant vicar?

Beg pardon?

Did you hear an elephant just then?

You've just had the needle haven't you old chap - takes a while to get over it. It could produce auditory something or other but then I'm not a doctor thank God!

As the sound came again if anything louder, wilder, Fettle beckoned for the dinghy, and was soon ashore begging his pardon and raising his cap as he left the party. Hedge jumped up. To follow. But missed the dinghy. He jumped and landed on the wheelchair boat tipping the rigid Plerns into the water. Hedge with another leap was clear of the water onto the poolside. He hurried out after the doctor. In the tubular corridor Hedge could hear the trumpeting louder. The corridor was long with concave doors leading off. The inspector hurried along not sure where the doctor had gone. Then he heard a crash. The other way. He turned about and ran towards the noise. Louder - a bellowing trumpet - certainly an elephant - and crashing and shattering - where was it coming from? There was the lab. Door. As Hedge reached for the handle the noise abruptly stopped. The door was locked. No it wasn't. And he pushed it open and entered the big laboratory that was now an absolute wreck. Midst the mess stood Belcher, and over in the corner was Fettle. Fettle lit a small cheroot.

The elephants - where are the elephants? demanded Hedge.

Elephants?

The elephant then doctor?

You've got an elephant syndrome old chap - worry - nerves...

This mess?

I'm afraid our Belcher threw a bit of a fit - tantrum - he wasn't much noticed at the ball.

Belcher dragged his foot amongst the broken glass.

White Power, he muttered, that's all I want - White Power.

You're not getting any White Power, Belcher - you're White Trailer Trash - get that into your head, said Doctor Fettle.

That's even better, said Nurse Belcher. Thanks so much for that.

Hedge realised that this was an act put on for him. A cover-up. It was then he noticed what can only be described as after the Lord Mayor's show. A piece of elephant dung. You couldn't blame everything on Belcher.

CHAPTER XIV

The next morning Hedge walked in the nursing home grounds. He was still waiting for his wretched bug clearance. Drag. Never been on such a case. The doctor seemed in no hurry. But if they were all dying off like flies within a fortnight he'd be hard pushed to get a preliminary report in. Very unsatisfactory. Yes there was the chapel tucked away over there. No sign of the Ku Klux Klan. Strange goings on. Still the vicar did seem to go with the rest of the place. Deliberately odd as if they were putting on a show to convince him that he was hallucinating...

He backed away and stared. Coming down the drive was - what? He ducked behind a bush. There was Doctor Fettle and pushing a stretcher trolley the rat white power fink Belcher. Trailer Trash right on! I hate him! Homophobia? Outlawed in the Force nowadays we all had to adjust. Reorientation. Find the female within yourself and celebrate her that was a bit rich but it made for a nice weekend course in the country with the chaps. No, this hatred was personal. Belcher had his partner the inflatable Doris and what? What? Yes what was he doing with her for it seemed his tastes ran to playing games with her as well. Don't go typecasting anyone, Hedge told himself. You don't know who the villains are these days. Now take the Super what was he up to contacting Fettle? Were they all in it together? Anyway the Super wanted him to know that he was in on the farcical birthday celebrations.   What was the degree of interconnection? What did Hedge mean? Who was he? Who? Pay attention, don't slip! Here they come...

What were they up to? He peered through the bushes...

Down the drive they came. The fool Fettle had on a white tropical suit and carried an umbrella to shield him from the sun. At this time of year I ask you? Perhaps he liked dressing up. Down they came, past him, feet crunching in the gravel. Here – Belcher the pig was barefoot. A penance? On the trolley was a beautiful boy lying exposed to the sun from the neck up, but covered elsewhere with a blanket. What was wrong with the poor lad? What were they doing to him? They came to the gates, and yes, Fettle made Belcher give him a key from that damn chain - you've never seen such a fuss - fink! And then the doc undid the padlock - so they locked the place up - getting in and out was not meant to be easy at least it made clear it was private property forbidden ground. They pushed the stretcher out into the road running by the clinic. Hey. Belcher tipped up the trolley and the lad slid off onto the road and lay there in a crumpled heap. Belcher collected the blanket and dusted off his hands. Job done. Fettle looked on in full composure from under his umbrella. The medical party withdrew leaving the poor lad   and relocked the iron gates. That's no way to discharge a patient. The poor demented fool. Probably a young hippy or something gone astray. Hedge would like to give him some advice. Fettle and Belcher disappeared up the drive into the building. Hedge went towards the gate. But the lad had vanished. Hedge was disappointed. He had no-one to give his advice to now. He turned away from the gate and there was the lad standing under a tree.

Oih!

What?

Well - you - can't wander round like that - in your pyjamas - you mean they just bundle you out just like that?

They said I was better.

What?

Like they've got to have a quick turnover of beds an' they?

Yes but…

I 'spect they'll send me clothes on.

Highly unsatisfactory young man - take my word for it - I'm a man of the world.

Yers.

Anyway you're back in - come back for your clothes have you?

Not likely mate - I'm spying on 'em - I've got something on 'em I 'ave.

Ahhh. The inspector looked interested. Have you got a mirror?

The lad didn't have a mirror but Hedge remembered he had a small hand mirror for emergencies and he took a peek in it. Yes he did look interested.

Continue, said the inspector, determined to keep that interested look on his face for he wanted to entice the lad's story but he looked more determined than interested. Damn that. Don't slip. Keep it real…

Out with it lad - come on - I should warn you I'm an officer of the law - that is of the law of the land - you get my meaning?

Well, said the young lad, looking quite radiant, it's elephants an' it?

Hedge was amazed, so young. Yet could he know it all? Hedge was tempted to blow his whistle but didn't want to frighten the lad. Time for celebration later. Go on…

Well - that's it aren't it - elephants - I mean er - like they shouldn't do that to elephants.

Do what to elephants my boy?

Carve 'em up like.

So he knew. The lad confirmed Hedge's sanity and gave him confidence in his enquiries. It was not the effect of the needle. Well not altogether. Something was going on elephant-wise and this little lad had a clue. His hair was golden and showered round his head throwing off the sun's light. He was more than pretty. Pretty pretty like that rat Belcher. No the boy was beautiful.

You've got a cheeky face you have.

Gets me into trouble.

It'll pay you to co-operate - I'll make it as easy as I can for you.

Don't care much.

Just then the lad pointed, and his mouth opened.

You've got good teeth, said Inspector Hedge.

Look.

Inspector Hedge followed the lad's finger. There - in the sky. Heavens. Oh no. Floating over the trees was the inflatable policewoman. That rat fink swine that done up to kill tart had overdone it this time.

Hedge knew he loved Doris, so named, his inflatable Wonder Woman. Admit it.

Swine! He yelled. Look what he's done to her! He's over-pumped her! He'll pay for this that white trash tart!

What is it? said the lad.

The inspector was overcome. Yes there was the knicker-faced Belcher running from cover with the bicycle pump. He could only have been a moment in the building before he sneaked out with her into the grounds to have his way with her. But she had got away floating high that was the good news.

Ah! There you go! yelled Hedge. And indeed Belcher went. Straight into the building by some devious side entrance - rathole - whatever.

Hedge could not pursue. He drew out a revolver. Then took out a bullet. Then a form pad. He jotted down a few details hurriedly.

Keep sight of her, he said. Name of Doris.

Righto, said the lad. 'Ere she's going right out the grounds…

Hang on - hang on - hang on - forms forms forms - sign here lad - witness, lucky you're here - watch for the empty cartridge - we've got to save the cartridge.

What you going to do?

Shoot her.

You can't do that.

What after what that swine's done to her? What use is she to me now?

Not her fault is it?

No. Hedge aimed steady at his beloved. Only now he knew what he would have to do - and that he loved her. In this moment he knew - and a tear trickled down his face. Could he do it? But he'd signed the form. Done in triplicate. It would take ages to sort out that mess. He squeezed the trigger. Quick. Simple. She flew on.

Blast! Quick where's the forms? As he reached for the pad they heard another gunshot. And she - ahh the inflatable lovely - oh dear - there she went sighing to earth. Someone else had done the dirty work. Inspector Hedge had a lifelong enemy. If he could find him.

You could mend the puncture, said the lad. 'Ere come on let's find 'er.

It wouldn't be the same…

Don't be a burke. You'd hardly notice the difference.

Her patched up?

Come on…

They went through the small copse of trees behind which she had disappeared. There. There she was. Caught in the uppermost branches of an elm tree. It was a rookery, and the rooks cawed round - an awful racket as they scoured the sky - black.

Heavens, said Hedge, I'm not up to it.

I'll get her down for you.

No.

Yers.

No - save your pretty neck lad - it's too dangerous - leave it - she'll be happier up there.

And he turned away. For truth to tell he was overcome. And murder grew in his heart. He had been outwitted. Outclassed. The elephants. Her. Which was Doris. The lot. The boy seemed good. So perhaps he - the Inspector - authentic ringing true what you see is what you get no monkey business - the sole representative of law and order - was not entirely on his own.

I'd appreciate your help, said Hedge. Not that there's anything in it for you.

Sure, said the lad, I an' got anything to do - I never 'ave…

What?

'Ad much to do like.

Have you heard of the incurables my boy?

No sir - why you're not one of 'em are yer?

I wonder sometimes, said Hedge, and took the lad's hand for a moment.

Yes - thanks for the offer lad. Comradeship. Like in the trenches.

Ere leave off. Ain't you well like? Is that it?

What? No…

Focus, Hedge, focus. He squinted. In the sunlight…

I am…

That's good, mate.

I… am…listen…can you hear anything?

Ears pricked the boy not so young as first imagined and definitely an odd one waited the cawing of the crows turned to silence…

…A bit distracted at the moment, said Hedge, and wandered off through the copse. The lad trailed after him.

CHAPTER XV

I love that boy, thought Hedge. It was a noble love. Worthy of a police officer. Though the Yard seemed far away these days. You get involved sometimes in a case. It is a foreign shore, put a message in a bottle and cast it into the sea. Don't forget me. He had no way to contact his superiors. Superiors. Let 'em rot. Yes - let 'em. He was the man on the beat. Front Line where it counted. His heart got broken twice a day. Not them. I'm a number to them. But I'll do my duty despite those buggers. Always laughing at you behind your back. To hell with 'em. He'd like to adopt the boy some time later but didn't know how to go about this matter. He'd not adopted a boy before. Better late than never. He'd asked. He had asked - if he had a family - the lad? Had he? Yes the boy had answered wolves in the forest.

Wolves?

Maybe, said the lad. There were some people but they were very offhand. Earlier like.

Earlier?

Yeah. Earlier. Then it gets all fuzzy like. Like I was running and she couldn't find me.

Your Mum?

Do you fink so? That's interesting.

Have you got a family?

I don't know. Why are you asking?

It could be an obstacle, said Hedge. They might object to your being adopted.

They never 'ave before, he said.

Are you too old to be adopted?

I could be, said the lad. It's not for me to decide.

Strictly speaking, said Hedge, you should be an orphan first.

Oh we can't wait for all that. I'm fed up wiv 'em I am - families! I've had lots of 'em - what they ever done for me?

I'll have a word with the Super when I get back - he knows the law inside out - and watch your aitches.

Yes sir, said the lad.

They might team up later, him and the lad. When the boy was a bit older. After he'd had some education. Inspector Hedge could go private one day, he thought, cos Inspector Hedge is not much liked at the Yard, is he? No, someone is blocking his advancement given his brilliant record, Inspector Class Two? He should be Class One and he wasn't just thinking about the money. He'd hit a brick wall of prejudice against his talent, his unconventional way of solving cases - they were all jealous. Well him and the lad could start an agency. They could investigate all these rotten divorces. That's why he'd never got married.

You mean again because you were married once and where does a sentence end? Once upon a time. A childless relationship. Was that a marriage? Alice. Another story...

It was lonely without a boy - a son really - if it wasn't too late - he'd like to make something of the lad. The cadets at Hendon when he was younger starting out - they didn't like him much either - at Hendon - probably cos he worked too hard... But the boy was a loner that was clear and would probably stray off sometime - and break his heart - but there what is a heart if it cannot be broken?

I'll speak to the Vicar, he said to the lad. He might know something about adoption.

They were hiding in a coal cellar. Or coke. Could be a smokeless zone. The point was - what was the point? Keep the boy out of Fettle's way.

What's your name then?

Ned.

And Ned it shall be, said Hedge rather foolishly. Tell me - Ned - what do you know about the elephants?

Well they're like in a big field like an' they - an' you seen 'em - underground - an' I was having a look roun' like - an' I go in this lab like - see - an' I see - they got an elephant in there - an' they - an' they got these electrodes an' they? Tied to 'is 'ead like...

Watch your aitches.

An so they're givin'...

And your Gs...

Giv'n this 'ole poor elephant an' they the ole shock treatment - the ole ECT - I thought they saved that for humans...

Have you been done?

Oh yeah - it's...like what? It's the elephants I worry about - cos I'm rubbish like eh...

No.

But an elephant is a thing of beauty - tan' rubbish like what I am - I don't care wot they do to me - cos I 'ate 'em - they can't hurt me like - but an elephant an' got no hatred in 'im. An' they turn on the electricity dun they - an I'm watching - there was all hell let loose - thank Gawd!

When was this?

'Bout free days ago.

Three days, corrected Hedge.

Look if you wanna tell the story...

Listen lad I'm trying to teach you as you go along - don't be cheeky. So then what?

Wot?

What happened?

I give up.

Don't give up lad. You never give up, right? Right?

The boy scratched his head looking bemused mouth slightly ajar - vacant - was there going to be any more info coming from this source? No. Yes. Go on...

Right. Yeah... Like they must have had another go with the elephants the night of the flotilla ball. Well I been drugged - I was out - like they din' know - they din' fink I knew - rubbish like me like - but they knew I - I...

What?

I forget. The lad clutched his head. I dint used to forget - now I forget - sometimes - forget I 'ate 'em - I forget - like - like...

The lad looked frightened.

Careful, said Hedge gently. Take it easy sonny - you've got plenty of time to remember now - all the time in the world...

I remember - I 'ate 'em.

Mind those aitches Ned - I'll never let you answer the phone - eh?

Hedge laughed and the boy smiled cautiously like the sun coming out from behind a cloud.

They didn't know that you knew about the elephants then?

Oh no.

Very well lad. You stay here 'cos I've got to go back to the ward - my ward - to keep things looking hunky dory - right?

No...

What do you mean, no?

I mean - yes. Like what's the difference?

Between no and yes? Why did you come back?

I ain't got anywhere else to go like. I decided to investigate.

Investigate eh? That sounds like a cop to me. You've got the makings son. Now you get your head down and have a rest. Stay here, right? Don't take the initiative. Do as you're told and you'll come to no harm.

Alright...

Right?

As long as you care 'bout the elephants as well?

When we go boy, said Hedge, standing at the door of the cellar, we go together - elephants and all, got it?

Hedge felt ten feet tall as he stepped back into the grounds furtively. The lad believed him. Believed in him. He had someone else in his life now. How he was going to get the elephants four stories up to the surface he didn't know. but if someone got them down there - he would get them up again.

CHAPTER XVI

It was the vicar who had shot the inflatable policewoman out of the sky. Full of curiosity he stood at the bottom of the tree and stared up at topmost branches in which she was entangled. How could he retrieve her, this mysterious female flying object? Perhaps she was from Mars. He had nearly phoned the Air Ministry - like a lot of things he had nearly done - but had decided to tackle this one himself. He had been out in the grounds shooting pheasant and other wild life for Harvest Festival. The vicar hitched up his cassock and tried to shin up the tree. it was heavy going although he got to a height which quite frightened him. The wind stirred and she - ahh the deflated one - drifted to earth. The vicar let go and landed in a heap beside her. He picked up the rubber affair - bewildered - stirred by emotions he could not fathom - and scuttled off with her towards the chapel.

Inside the ward, in the cubicle, Inspector Hedge remembered the envelope. It was his only real clue and to tell the truth he had been saving it - he needed a treat. Perhaps now - go on, spoil yourself. He carefully prised the envelope open and pulled out several newspaper clippings. They all related to the disappearance of an aircraft and the lost scientists. He noticed the date on the clippings. Yes that was today's date. But he'd had the envelope in his possession since yesterday. Who was manufacturing evidence?

Shirley peeped out of the coal cellar door. It had always been a game with her to pretend to be a boy. A bit old for that now but it was so easy in her case. A talent. Look it was her job. Boy or girl. Like a lot of other decisions you made them up as you went along and you stayed alive...

She had heard a noise - a rumbling of heavy transport - and disobeying the commands of her new friend to stay hidden in the cellar - who was he to throw his weight round anyway - her mind stayed in the role difficult to shake off - she moved away from the door into the dusk and made for a clump of bushes. Through these she peered. A big lorry some way off was backing off the drive towards her. It stopped. A mechanical noise assailed her ears and the turf lifted before her revealing a big trap to an underground facility. Correction - the underground facility. A crane rose up from the earth and swung round over the lorry. The crane was attached to a crate. The crate was winched up and swung over the trap. Inside the crate she could see several kangaroos. They looked happy enough but they were poor dumb creatures and could not expect to realise the perils of the underground park into which they were being lowered, disappearing from view. Next was unloaded a statue of Prince Albert which was also lowered into the bowels of the earth. The trap closed and the lorry drove onto the driveway then down and out of the gates. The gates were closed and locked behind the vehicle. A peacock screeched somewhere. It was a pleasant evening becoming a quiet night in the peaceful atmosphere of the English countryside.

CHAPTER XVII

They were in Doctor Fettles office which was not in the lift which Inspector Hedge found peculiar.

The Public have been fooled, he declared. How do you respond to that?

True, said Doctor Fettle. And not for the first time. But it is not in the Public's interest always to know the truth. They would be filled with fear and dread if they knew the wretched effects of this bug. The outcry would be tremendous, Inspector! And bring down Governments. Is that what we want? Civil disobedience? Rioting in the street?

The dance of death due to the plague you mean?

Oh dear, could it be that bad? Yes I suppose it could. Sincerity vibrated in the vocal chords of the doctor. He was cooperating. Imagine the reaction even were it known that five men were awaiting death as a result of their patriotic work in germ warfare.

Four men, said the inspector.

Five men were waiting, answered Fettle. Until the murder that is. The pointless - but is it pointless that's for you decide - farcical killing. Why?

You have the brain for it. I don't. The whole damn operation was supposed to be hush hush - they the incurables are dedicated men and took the hard path - they knew the risks - they were sworn to secrecy - they signed the Act - they knew the consequences of Emergency plan B. If the worst came to the worst they were to disappear from the face of this earth. And that's what they've done...

In a plane crash that never happened, said Hedge. So they could be tucked away underground here to perish and their remains safely disposed of.

You found the envelope then?

As planted, Doctor. In your desk.

We provide the information that we are instructed to. To help you with your enquiries.

And who would you say I am? As a matter of interest?

That is the question, yes.

Patient or policeman? In your mind?

My mind is adrift with images and stories and fancies and facts and they pass, dear Inspector, like - like clouds in a blue sky. With sudden storm bursts from swollen banks of doubt. But then my mind is hardly the subject of this enquiry, is it?

I'm thinking, said Inspector Hedge. The cost of a cover-up could be worse than warning the Public now - today - and preparing as best we can for a possible outbreak of the Black Plague.

With its ravaging effect? London gone? What antidote have we, my dear Inspector?

You're trying an antidote on me? What? Could you not - that is the National Health Service - mass vaccinate or inoculate the Public?

Please, Inspector Hedge. We are small cogs in the wheels of the State that grind exceeding small. We only know what we are told. The rest is surmise. This could be a gigantic exercise for instance!

But the incurables will die?

Doubtless. We have established that. National Security must exercise itself from time to time.

You mean it was not...?

My life is devoid of meaning Jack? Yes, Jack. And I am Ian. Am I Ian? You decide. Yes I look at you Jack and I think - many things. In the ward - in the ward itself life takes on a different meaning - and strangely enough - how strange it all is - given the circumstances there was a terrible hue-and-cry over this pointless murder. My dear Inspector I tried to explain to them the sheer irrelevance of the - you know that's what it is - but would they listen? No. It was like dressing for dinner as far as they were concerned, the decencies still had to be observed. They were Englishmen. Well British. A way of life was at stake, something foreigners would not necessarily understand. So it was decided after consultation with the Yard to call you in.

Why wasn't I briefed properly - if I take your word? Instead of leaving clues for me to pilfer from your desk drawer?

Good point. Why spoil the fun? . Actually I was asked to profile you. Your loyalty factor registered seven - out of ten - and we needed a nine. But other factors weighed heavily in your favour - your ability to crack a case however bizarre - so I am told - so I am told - and loyalty is a fluid entity hard to assess, is it not the Praetorian Guard, those closest to the Ruler who are the most danger to the Throne? They sent you here on the understanding that I would do a few tests - psychological - anonymously - you'd hardly notice, don't worry you sailed through. Regraded to a nine Inspector Hedge, congratulations...

Thanks, he said. Let's put that to one side. You said this could be part of a Government exercise, right? Where people die? You expect me to swallow that?

What do we know, Jack? From time to time the State heaves up out of the deep like a leviathan creature -it is the worst monster imaginable! It must spew up its blackening bile upon the ocean and cast the plague it bears upon golden beaches...

Spare me your rhetoric, Doctor.

You have to decide for yourself, Jack my lad - do call me Ian. Or call me George if you like! Or Aladdin! Do we not enter a magic cave? On a daily basis?

Hedge stared at the doctor. What's your point?

My dear Inspector the point is do you want to - that is are you prepared to - to go in - into the isolation unit - the Incurable Ward - now that you know the dangers?

That is between me and my department, said Hedge. The decision was made before I got here. I'm going in.

He represented Law and Order. There was no corner of the land where it was not reachable. He had been waiting all day for his clearance bug-wise. Did he really need this deliberately confusing conversation with the doctor about a Government exercise? The more tales they spin the more confusing it was meant to become. To lose him in the forest with no trail of breadcrumbs to lead him out again. Meanwhile he waited. Dawdling. Foot dragging. Concentrate on this interview...

Where did you get the serum from? asked Hedge. The one you injected me with?

Ernie.

Ernie? The corpse?

The only available source, old man.

I don't like that much, said Hedge.

He felt he had been properly mucked about. Almost controlled. Like an experiment. For heaven's sake they only had to tell him what they knew and he would do his job. Who could doubt his loyalty? His patriotism? He didn't need psychological profiles. It was enough to make him lose faith in them. Them. What faith he had left that is.   Regraded as a Loyalty Nine I suppose that was some use. Concentrate...

Why the murder? Have you any ideas on the subject, Doctor?

My field is medicine, Inspector. But this reeks of attention seeking, this murder to me. After all who would not want attention buried forty foot underground with no living options left?

A siren sounded, wailing through the building and disturbing the interview.

What's that? Said Hedge.

Chemical Police alarm.

Pardon?

Staff shortages old chap - all done by chemicals - control of patients etc - it's less brutal really - no truncheons - well in our case straightjackets - a chemical police agent release - thank God we live in civilised times.

Belcher burst in. Hedge nearly vomited but controlled his reaction to the nurse.

It's the incurables, Doctor!

What about them, Belcher?

Threatening to break the place up they are! A precipitous riot we have on our hands Doctor! I wouldn't lie to you!

Try CS5.

Right...

And Belcher...

Doctor?

We do have an intercom you know.

Oh I like a good trip round the corridors - good for the figure keeps you young - Oh my Gawd, right - it's all go today - CS5 right - medium?

Medium high, instructed the doctor.

Righty-ho! Toddle-pip!

Hedge watched her go, biting his lip.

The doctor said, They get restless you know, those incurables. Even if they stay loyal to Queen an Country the strain waiting to die must be intolerable. They're good chaps but they have to let off steam now and again.

Do they ever try and leave the ward? Asked Hedge.

That can be a problem, yes - it is a matter of chemical control really - the toxic aerosol supply.

You control the air quality?

Very much so. We can't be running in there and giving them all injections. It would be like a rugby match! And let it be said the incurables are an ideal subject.

What for?

For us to experiment on the uses of chemical policing. It can't do them any real harm given their very limited lifespan.

You could let them live out their last few days in peace surely? Suggested the inspector.

That's the whole idea of CS5 my dear chap.

The sirens stopped.

Belcher seems to have brought affairs under control. Good man, Nurse Belcher. Invaluable... The doctor looked at the inspector quizzically. Do I detect - forgive my asking - a note of hostility in your dealings with my head nurse?

All are suspect and all are innocent until proved guilty, answered Hedge. My personal feelings about people are not relevant.

Well, cooed the doctor, well well... I am not so sure about that. You come across as being rather homophobic, Inspector.

I have been on Away Days with the boys and girls in Blue, don't you worry about that. We are up to speed on this subject. We are not in the Stone Age, don't worry. It has been dealt with.

Only such hostility - which I did notice - and for which you are not to blame - could be an outward sign of suppression of your own sexuality.

I have not come here to discuss my sexuality, doctor. But to investigate a criminal case. Inspector Hedge's voice was tightly controlled, suggesting he was rattled.

My door is always open, my dear Inspector. Pop in and feel free to discuss anything that's on your mind.

Hedge was breathing heavily. He was being got at. The head nurse was a fairy, OK leave it at that. But... What about Doris? He'd got his hands on his Policewoman Inflatable - his partner hadn't he? That was another matter that he would settle in his own time with the lovely provocative scented Nurse Belcher.

There was a buzzing noise. Doctor Fettle had a message. He took out his intercom device and read what was upon the screen.

Excellent news, he said. You're positive Inspector Hedge. It was a take factor - your injection my dear fellow. You can proceed with your enquiries.

What?

You are free to enter the incurable ward. Isn't that good news?

CHAPTER XVIII

Doctor Fettle and Inspector Hedge stepped out of the lift at Minus 4.

There was no springboard to the pool. That was Minus 3. Unless it was an hallucination, thought Hedge. The injection to immunise him against the bug, Code name Green Swan, might have had unknown side effects in which case it would be left to him to work what was real and what was fevered imagination - as if the case were not difficult enough. The doctor was useless, or devious, in the pay of a Government agency - as was he - so who was orchestrating the whole damn thing?

Was it not a vanity to think that anyone was in charge? Everyone in their own corner securing their pension rights! However...

Oh dear, said Doctor Fettle. We've arrived at dinner time. Better not to go in while they're feeding. They can be dangerous. Snappy, you know. The food means a lot to them.

An orderly was taking trays from a trolley and placing them onto a conveyor belt that moved the dinners through a flap - and supposedly a sterilisation chamber - thence into the ward. A patient was taking the trays from the conveyor belt in the ward and placing them on another trolley.

That's Morgan, said the doctor. Can be a trouble-maker - barrack room lawyer type - knows his rights you know the sort...

He looks quite placid at the moment, said Hedge.

Thanks to the CS5 spray. We had to introduce that or they'd be throwing their trays all over the place. Don't be fooled by the calm. I wouldn't go in there myself.

Does nobody go in the ward?

Only the vicar - and he's crazy.

But Doctor, how do you administer to their needs?

Oh it's all self-contained you know.

But medically?

Oh occasionally I shove a few bottles through you know - pills and stuff - medicines, you're right - and progress charts, updates - anything to give them the impression that they're cared for not abandoned - they're intelligent chaps they know what's going on - but they also cherish the illusion - much as we do on the outside here wouldn't you say - but to a different time scale admittedly.

Hedge stared into the ward. Another patient was sitting at a table holding a knife and fork probably salivating. One sat on his bed in a floral dressing gown reading a magazine. And the last one was in a corner doing press-ups. At last he - a representative of law and order - was going in there to interview the patients. A vital step in his enquires and something that he had been looking forward to - getting on with the job - just get on with it! But now - dread - yes a fear gnawed his stomach. He was entering the unknown and still had a feeling that somewhere he was being set up - sold down the river. There was only one way to find out. Press on and deal with the consequences as they turned up...

How long will this vaccine be effective? Asked Hedge.

Who said it's effective? said Fettle bluntly. That's something we'll find out. It's you that insists upon interviewing these patients - you could do it from the outside by intercom - no-one's forcing you to go in there.

And no-one's stopping me either. I've got a job to do and that is the scene of the crime. The vaccine has worked for the vicar, hasn't it?

So far, said the doctor. Speak of the devil, here he comes.

It was indeed the vicar who had arrived in his plastic mac and gum boots.

Hello! Hello everyone! Freedom lovers everywhere! Know you the breath of Spirit - the wind of Heaven that blows where it will and casts out the cobwebs of doubt!

I wouldn't go in there during feeding time, advised Doctor Fettle.

Even with the raiment of Light - my shield and buckler - I would not do that. What are they having for afters?

Chocolate pudding.

Mmmm - I might try a bit of Christianity on them after that - they'll be in a good mood to tolerate me. Oh dear, start as you mean to carry on - the message - the message yes indeed! Inspector, do you believe in the bug?

Why yes...

Then you might be saved, said the vicar simply, though it must be said the meaning was enigmatic. Have you been told the truth about this affair here? This mess? This Government mess-up?

I'm here on a case, Vicar.

A case is it? It's murder plain and simple, my good man. It's a crucifixion really. Lambs to the slaughter. And I must guide these souls to paradise if it be possible. It amazes me the hardness of heart in the face of death - the obstinacy! But of course I'm dealing with scientists - materialists hoist by their own petard through this wretched affair...

Have you finished Vicar? said Doctor Fettle.

Who killed Ernie, said the vicar. And one may ask - who is next? We are all on the brink of eternity - especially in this wretched place. I hate your rational thinking , Doctor. You are more lost than any soul I have met. I will not struggle with Satan to win you back, hark me - I must go to more fruitful pastures and let you go where you will - damn rationalists I say!

Doctor Fettle smiled. I was a Stalinist last week.

You serve the State and I serve the Almighty - the Invisible...

Now don't get upset, Ian, in front of our guest, suggested Fettle.

Oh Trevor, I have to let you go...

But surely I am Ian and you are Trevor?

Have it your own way. What's in a name? I'll smell as sweet.

Whilst Inspector Hedge was noting this exchange there was a disturbance along the corridor. Belcher was coming along on a powered electric goods trolley.

The Belcher cometh! declared the vicar.

Make way! Make way for the parade! Cried out Belcher gaily, dragging his foot a little against the linoleum. I'm coming through!

Halt! commanded Doctor Fettle.

Belcher came to a halt. What's this? a roadblock?

What on earth have you got there, Nurse?

The box sir! You know - the box we ordered!

On the electric trolley was a large oblong crate marked EXPORT, FRAGILE and THIS WAY UP. Plus HANDLE WITH CARE - URGENT.

Where's he taking that? demanded Inspector Hedge.

Silly to make a mystery of it my dear chap. To the morgue.

Why? What's in it?

Frankly, Inspector, there is nothing in that crate at present. But there will be when we put Ernie into it. Carry on Belcher.

Hang on, said Hedge.

That's if it's alright by you?

It's not alright by me, Doctor. Oh no. You hang on a minute. That corpse is evidence. You can't export it.

We've got the license from the Ministry of Trade. I'm afraid that you are too late to object.

Could Hedge fight bureaucracy? Paperwork? The paperwork was all in order? To export the one piece of evidence he had. Well the second - the first being the letter with the forged newspaper clippings.

Where do you think you're exporting Ernie to?

He's going to the highest bidder, old chap. Which happens to be the Mighty Dollar. I'm glad we are able to play our part in rescuing the economy, eh Belcher?

I wish someone would recuse my economy, dear , simpered the head nurse.

You mean you are sending Ernie to America? demanded Hedge.

Yes, of course. We really have no choice in the matter- and nor do you.

It's a germ warfare swop, is it?

Fettle's lips tightened. I don't know the intricacies of the deal, Inspector. I do know that the corpse of Ernie...

God bless him, interjected the vicar. Just to let you know I'm still here. Still relevant.

The corpse of Ernie is an ideal container for the bug, continued the doctor. In fact the corpse is the safest way we know of transportation of the bug. Virus. Whatever bacterial presence it happens to be. Send the body off in a sealed chamber. Let the Yanks extract whatever it is - whatever it proves to be - from the corpse. It saves us from an awfully risky procedure - for which we have little precedent, eh Belcher?

Oh don't keep asking me, dear. I'm only here to make up the numbers.

You play the fool, Nurse Belcher. It keeps us going. I thank you for that.

Thank you, Doctor. Belcher gave a little curtsy.

So the Americans will extract a bug serum? Asked Hedge.

Hopefully. The bug is still active - alive - as was proved by what we were able to take out, modify, and inject into you - giving you hopefully an immunity to the disease. But don't count on it. I mean if you want to wait until the Americans have produced their vaccine...?

That could be months.

You could come back...

I'm not coming back! exploded the inspector. I'm here, I'm getting on with the job!

Well I better go and say the last rites for Ernie, said the vicar. I didn't know he was for export.

Belcher said, Hop aboard, Vicar. No need to walk.

The vicar climbed up beside Belcher on the platform at the the rear of the electric trolley and they sailed silently away down the passage and through the swing doors.

Hedge said, A joke's a joke and this has gone far enough. You cannot export a body - a prime piece of evidence upon which we await an autopsy result, may I remind you, Doctor - in the middle of a bloody murder enquiry!

If only those rules applied, Inspector, down here - we'd all be happy. Fettle squeezed his arm and for a moment Hedge thought he detected a note of pain in the doctor's voice. Unfortunately that is not how it is in today's world where we are put and where we stand.

How could he, Hedge, get in touch with the Yard and check this latest development? He couldn't go through the doctor, the man was too unreliable. Corrupted even. Gone bad. A step at a time - slipping down the ladder rung by rung - the doctor's moral compass had dropped into the depths and been smashed. Any vestiges of decency in Fettle were merely a remembered sentiment. Still clutching his arm Doctor Fettle started walking Hedge away. Come along...

What about the incurables?

Upon the observation window a steel shutter slid down and shut out sight of the incurables.

This is not the time, Inspector. They must rest and so must you. You have more information to digest while they digest their dinners.

There was a medical station with a desk and two chairs.

Do sit down, Inspector.

Hedge was not feeling so well himself now he thought about it. His energy flared up like straw in a fire and was gone the next minute. Never mind. he would sit down. Ever since that injection...

Here drink this. It will buck you up. Doctor Fettle was offering him a paper cup containing a crimson fluid.

Thanks. He did not drink it immediately. This is all very Alice In Wonderland, he said.

Fettle laughed. Sorry about that. Outside my control. Do drink up - it won't harm you - I know you're having a problem trusting anyone - but that happened believe me long before you came here. I am actually on your side. I don't mean all that baloney about law and order. That's your business and you're welcome to it. The doctor was sitting behind the desk his feet up, twiddling with a biro pen.

... I mean you personally, OK? Because that's all that's left. You haven't got there yet, I realise. But you will - get to that point - of survival - when you realise how much you're being used.

Who by? said Hedge.

The whole damn system, Inspector. It's rotten from top to bottom.

Hedge drank the medicine. It might make him feel better. He

squashed the paper cup in his hand. I could do with a little lie down. I'll have a rest in my room.

I'm frightfully sorry, said the doctor. We're having it redecorated.

What? Hedge was confused. Hung up. A great lassitude was upon him. I'll be able to have it back afterwards. The room?

Certainly - if you are staying?

It's a bed - I've got to kip down somewhere. Look here, I... He did feel so damn tired. Hard to concentrate. Have you got a phone? Where is it?

It's cut off, old chap. Trouble is - police or someone tapping - Security Services, MI5. We don't know who's turf this is supposed to be - and nor do they, I fancy. Anyway. Yes...All our communication is done by pigeon.

Pigeon? Pigeon? Was the potion he had just taken helping any? Carrier pigeons to the Yard? Scotland?

No to Trafalgar Square. In the first place our carrier pigeons go there - where they can mix with the other pigeons un-noticed - until we - meaning them - they - the recipients...

Yes, well how do they sort it out with all those pigeons already there in the square?

With difficulty. What with all the tourists and photography. You know they've been cleaning the Old Man recently and that's no coincidence.

What? What old man? Hedge yawned mightily.

Nelson's Column. Where our birds are trained to perch up there - away from it all. Then we send - they send that is - good men with a head for heights up the column - pretending to be doing restorative work - to take the messages from the pigeons! It's that simple...

It did not sound simple to Hedge who was struggling to stay awake.

Can I get a message to the Inspector? This is important...

You are the Inspector.

To my Super? The Superintendent.

No - I'm afraid these steeplejacks only work a five-day week and it's Friday evening they've all gone home.

I'm up the creek without a paddle here...

Hedge was dying in a field in Belgium. Distant drums rolled and there were far shouts and the noise of cannon. And drifting smoke. But he was past all that. Lance-Corporal Hedge lay in the arms of the scarlet uniformed Captain Fettle.

I'm passing, he said. How many times must I die in this sodden field?

As many times as the tale is told, replied the Captain. None more, none less.

Tell me, sir, if you have the wisdom to answer or else be silent - am I both mother and father to my own brat?

The tale spins. The roles change. Not both at once.

I see...

You are father and mother to the world Jack, said Captain Fettle. And this be your favourite field to die. All stories lie in your heart. So consider if you would change your tale?

In the leaving of it, Captain?

Aye.

I have left it late. But of a thousand deaths in Belgium near Waterloo I will chose another. For the girl in the Square who is me and gives birth and the soldier boy who deserted her - neither am I today.

You ramble, Jack. In your passing please be gone for you confuse me your Captain and I am rudderless as it is without your distraction.

Can you get a message to my Nell, good Captain?

Not likely for the steeplejacks only work Monday to Friday, Jack. So the pigeons do not fly today. It is a Sunday. What use would be a message to your beloved wife Nell stuck up the top of Nelsons Column?

She's not stuck up Nelsons Column, sir, but she is far up the duff. It's our fifth brat overdue same as the rent.

Gold coins travel to your wife, Corporal. Even as we speak some six months pay lad.

That is done then. Restitution is paid and England be saved.

Aye, said the Captain weary of so many partings that day and the closing of so many youthful trusting eyes. So farewell, Jack...

Upon those words the good Captain for such he was flung his arms in the air to the sound of a shot which killed him through the head good and dead so he was gone to his next scene before Redcoat Corporal Jack who could only follow shortly. From such a role chosen from the litter of bodies left upon that sad field of Waterloo of which we speak to this day with pride. Is it true that we gather in clusters, none lost, all to play our parts from one dimension to the next? Aided by angels? Jack's eyes closed forever which needs an essay as he sank back into the bloodied bosom of his Captain. The day was done...

CHAPTER XVIX

When Hedge came to he had been put into a lounge. Well he assumed he had been put there because he had no knowledge of how he came to be in the room. It was more a conference room than a lounge he decided, based upon the fact that he was seated in a casual circle of easy chairs and as he awoke he was aware of other people talking. Coming into focus he wondered whether he should play mum and listen? Too late...

Ahh! said Doctor Fettle. The inspector is awake.

Hedge blinked. Opposite him sat Sir Hilary Spong and scattered in the circle about six other people.

Sorry I dozed off ladies and gentlemen, Hedge said. Though why he should be sorry he couldn't imagine.

This is a but hush hush old chap if you'd like to go back to sleep - but you're welcome to stay.

Had they interrupted his sleep or he interrupted their conference?

Look here, as far as I'm concerned...

Quite, said Doctor Fettle. You should be in on it. Ladies and gentlemen may I call you to order and ask you to stop muttering. I'd like to introduce Inspector Hedge who has just woken up from his dreams to join us. I did warn you of the consequence of holding our top secret meeting in this lounge while the poor man had his rest but but we were hardly going to walk the grounds.

There are other rooms available, stated Doctor Blossom, a name confirmed by her tag. She was fifty years old, thin and a sailor might say any port in a storm about how attractive she was.

All being fumigated, replied Fettle. And Inspector Hedge is having his room redecorated.

Can we afford it? An Indian gentleman spoke up. Mr Patel - Accounts.

Why is he having his room done up?

Because it was in puce green affecting his mental health.

We can't afford it.

Doctor Fettle smiled.We have a secret fund which is allocated to the care of the incurables and as they are killing each other and as Inspector Hedge is here to investigate this matter then I directed this fund for the redecoration of his room, number 22 - which needed doing anyway. The colour scheme was quite sickening and the special fund has to be used up so we are getting the room done for nothing.

Mr Patel nodded. In that case let us move the good inspector from room to room while he is here and redecorate the whole wing.

Agreed, said someone else. Next business.

I do not know who has decided that this gentleman from Scotland Yard should attend our gathering? I cannot believe it was chance... This from Doctor Summers - actually Busty Summers - when on more informal terms which could only be enjoyed on a summers night on a park bench. This is entirely a hush hush affair - is it not? To be settled amongst ourselves. And he is a stranger. The stranger! Proverbial and threatening he rides into town. We watch him as he descends from his horse. What is he doing in our midst we ask? Has he come to find one of us guilty - or maybe the whole lot of us - is he indeed the figure of retribution?

Look here, said Hedge, I'm no Clint Eastwood. What? I have no accompanying music neither do I whistle. I am not answerable to you lot. I'm on a case, right? True you are all probably guilty of some offence for guilt is the common lot of humanity. Which is why we never get the wrong man - though it may be for the wrong offence.

Well said! Sir Hilary called out. Now we have the Oedipal guilt of all established by the inspector we can move on!

The Inspector of our Souls, said Doctor Summers.

Please let us not get carried away, said Doctor Fettle. We must not become figurative or esoteric. We have urgent matters to decide and this simple police inspector is now involved with us. Unwittingly - let us face it - we in this room have become involved in a silent conspiracy the tentacles of which are spreading alarmingly. I fear that now is the last chance to speak up.

Here here! said someone.

I suggest that ' here here ' be omitted from the minutes of our meeting, said Doctor Blossom.

Here here, said someone else.

And that one too, she said, pointing a finger at the offender.

Shilly shallowing! Minnows! Shouted Fettle. Where are we going with this? To hell in a handcart! He sat down exhausted.

Sir Hilary said, The feeling of the meeting is to include the inspector.

Use him. Use him, muttered Fettle. Use every damn one of us to the last drop.

Sir Hilary turned to a doctor who had remained silent to this point. Professor Bunker. Your turn.

Professor Bunker arose and shuffled through some important looking papers. Professor Bunker was a large woman not to be toyed with even though she longed for it. Her body spread voluminously under flowing garments. All the men in this room are male chauvinist pigs, she announced.

Noted, said Doctor Fettle.

And seconded, added Sir Hilary Spong.

Moving on, said Professor Bunker, I have been examining the regulations from the Ministry of Agriculture and Fisheries re the export of meat. Strictly speaking...

Strictly, said Doctor Blossom.

Very strictly, said Sir Hilary. Naked in cages.

Strictly speaking, went on the Professor, if we could get Ernie classified as a carcass - he could not be taken out of the country - bad meat - dangerous...

My God, said Sir Hilary.

Keep him here, spoke up Doctor Summers. He is our Ernie.

Here we have it, said the Prof tapping her papers. Foot and mouth disease is covered for animals - it says here in black and white - forbidden movement out of the district - never mind the country!

Ernie does not have foot and mouth, said Doctor Fettle.

In the cocktail of his infection we do not know what Ernie has, said Sir Hilary. That's why we need to keep him here to find out. He's ours. We love him.

The Min of Defence are determined Ernie shall go to the Americans, said the Prof. It's a big pay day for the Treasury and it is a secret we can exchange to keep our special relationship with the Yanks.

Inspector Hedge could see it all laid out for him. Yet he was no nearer to solving the murder of Ernie. All this information was fogging the issue. Hold on, he said. This won't do. Ernie must not leave the country until a proper autopsy has been conducted.

That's a joke, said Doctor Summers. And on a summers night you must wonder who cares? For on a park bench was the first and last moment of promise. How far we have come from nature in the conquering of it. And in conquering nature we have have subdued our own natures. I am afraid that all is lost. The life spark is leaving us...

The Min of Defence have priority, interrupted Doctor Fettle abruptly. They are our paymasters now - let's face it - in the devilish arrangements into which we have sunk.

Export or die, said Sir Hilary. The economy must come first of course.

If we want to export Ernie there is a way, said Professor Bunker. We could have him tinned.

What? A stir of concern ran through the meeting.

Yes, we could have him canned.

Canned Ernie?

He was often canned when he was alive, said Sir Hilary.

Though, continued the Prof craftily, under the Canned Meat Act we can get the product examined and condemned.

Brilliant! Exclaimed Fettle. That way our research material remains in this country. They can't fight their own damn restrictions.

Putting Ernie into tins could be a dangerous process, said Doctor Blossom. We haven't done anything like it before.

If we can do it with beef we can do it with Ernie, said Doctor Summers. Corned Ernie.

It seems to me that a tin of Ernie should be sent to his relatives, said Hedge. A nice gesture.

Impossible! You would find nowhere on the face of this earth meat that contaminated.

I was not suggesting they give it to the cat - keep it on the mantelpiece.

That's a nice thought, said Fettle. But too risky.

Prof Bunker persevered, If we could get this whole matter under the auspices of the Min of Ag and Fish...

From the Min of Defence, said Doctor Blossom. Wouldn't the Min of Health take us? In extremis?

You must be joking, said Sir Hilary. It took them three years to get rid of us. Biological warfare is not in their budget.

Well that is all we have time for today ladies and gentlemen. Doctor Fettle rose from his chair. It is now a matter of your consciences to be examined in prayer to a random God who creates a multitude of chances that evolution may continue. The future of mankind is at stake but more importantly so are our careers. Good Day.

Hedge stood up as they brushed past him, some with words of encouragement. Don't give up, Inspector. Thank you for risking your life for a decent outcome to this mess. And...You're mad but it helps.

Only Doctor Fettle remained, waiting for him.

Now you see what we're up against, he said. They will talk endlessly. Anything to avoid making a decision for which they may be held responsible. So, what's next, my dear fellow?

CHAPTER XX

Inspector Hedge in his newly decorated room still hated the curtains with their kidney bowl pattern. He had not minded the washed out green walls which previously reminded him of the sea - the sea! Now it was pale blue the sky and birds hovering. What of his situation? Did he have one? How was his case proceeding? He was not fooled by the conference. It was a double bluff. If they were canning Ernie it was to get him out of the country - not to keep him in. Disguised as a consignment of corned beef it was too easy but a corpse in that incubator thing would attract attention. It boiled down to publicity. They were frightened that the Public would find out. Not that he cared. He had come to his room to change his socks - any excuse would do - to reassess his situation but again he told himself it was a matter of perception not how it was but how he looked at it - from what angle? Up close what did an elephant look like? The closer you got the less elephant you saw. Doctor Fettle was waiting to take him down again to Level 4, the Incurable Ward. This time he must get in. He seemed to remember - no - or was it true - yes - that Doctor Fettle had given him some potion prior to his falling asleep - a pickup. Or a putdown. The thing was he didn't know what it was. Or the needle. Potions and injections. Coming in and out of consciousness. And he worried about Nell.

But who was Nell?

He had no idea. Was the inspector in control or simply imagining it? Say he got down to the ward and felt dizzy again? Was his life a side effect of medication? He would really value a second opinion. He thought he could trust Sir Hilary Spong.

Talk of the devil!

A wall panel slid open and Sir Hilary stepped out. Careful, he said, lots of hush. Now let's see what that beast has been doing to you - kindly remove your shirt.

Hedge eagerly complied while Sir Hilary from his bag prepared a needle.

Not another injection?

Oh no, Inspector, this is to give me a blood sample. I want to see what that calculating monster Fettle has been pumping into you.

And he gave me some medicine, said Hedge. In a little paper cup. And pills.

Ouch.

You were not fooled by that conference I trust?

You bet not, said Hedge trying not to wince.

They don't know how to deal with you. Sir Hilary pulled out the needle. All done. Just remove your trousers - and cough.

Inspector Hedge lowered his trousers and coughed.

Are you married?

No.

It might be a good idea to wait until after the next General Election.

Why?

Tax reasons, said Sir Hilary. You can get dressed now.

Hedge pulled up his trousers.

All seems to be in order. Doctor Fettle - he is a surgeon of course you know that - my advice is don't let him near you with the knife. He hasn't removed anything so far has he?

No, I'm here on a case...

Nevertheless be warned, said Sir Hilary. Though on a serious note...

He smiled at the inspector.

Are you I touch with the Yard? asked Hedge.

Sir Hilary did not avoid the question and stared back at Hedge.

There are more fish here to fry than the one you know of - Good Day.

And he stepped back behind the panel and was gone. Hedge buttoned up his shirt. He felt reassured. He could have tested my heart. But Hedge did not believe he had a heart. Naming. Separating. That's what they did. There was something pounding away inside. This time he must get into the ward.

CHAPTER XXI

The vicar stood back and admired his handiwork. Yes this year Harvest Festival would swing. There taking pride of place upon the altar set about with fruit flowers and wild game was HER - the inflatable object - womanly - now earthbound. He had mended the puncture of this heavenly visitation. Was it the Virgin Mary in disguise? It's the thought that counts. It should pack 'em in anyway. He went up into the pulpit. There tucked away was a clever intercom. He buzzed. Fettle in his office answered.

Vicar One here.

You're the only one we've got - go on One.

It's looking lovely Doctor - swinging - now I wonder would the Inspector be taking communion before the Harvest Festival service?

Fettle controlled his anger. He did not like nature - let alone to celebrate it.

I'll see if I can get Hedge to take communion in the morning - I'll note that.

Splendid! Well I'll see if I can slip something in the wafer shall I?

Taken ill at a service? Won't that look suspicious?

It will look beautiful - a happening - I put some LSD in the wafers last week - man they were gone - Roger and out.

The Vicar replaced the receiver.

Doctor Fettle flicked off his intercom thoughtfully. he would have to watch the vicar. Loyal. But hysterical. There might come a time when...

CHAPTER XXII

The steel shutter slid up. Yes there were the INCURABLES. Much the same as ever. Listlessly moving around. Or languidly still in bed. Miseries. Hedge was inclined to agree. Who with? Himself for one. Those incurables were a bit of a bring down.

Well here goes, Inspector.

OK Doctor, let's go...

I'm not going in there old chap - you're very much on your own. As I've told you the Vicar chances it sometimes - but he has faith doesn't he? The armour of Light!

Faith? Chances it? But isn't he inoculated as well?

He was but he doesn't believe in it. I'd say your chances are sixty percent.

Which way?

In your favour of course. Or I wouldn't dream of letting you enter the ward.

You mean I've got a forty percent chance of catching the - the thing...?

The inspector stopped himself saying Code Name Green Swan. Who knew even that this file existed? Possibly Fettle. He could not be sure what he had said before to the doctor or imagined he had said.

Doctor Fettle scratched his head. It's hard to calculate actually without the experience of case histories.

What is?

Your percentage chance of not becoming infected.

So he, Inspector Hedge, the great man or not so great depending what day it was but he could ironically describe himself - up for that - was risking his life again - hardly as he wished - it seemed so unromantic - unnoticed - he couldn't burble on to the Super about an injection take factor. He'd got the needle and that was that.

The Doctor was talking to him. Look old fella - you enter through the clearance chamber - better make the routine clear - straight through in - simple procedure - but out it'll take about half an hour - blood sample check - a needle will come out and inject you from the wall you simply strap your arm in the right place...

Another...? Inspector Hedge swallowed his words. Oh no. His arm was getting sore. He wouldn't have any blood left soon. What a case. Felt more like a guinea pig.

At least I'm here, he said.

As opposed to...?

Somewhere else. I've shown up.

Yes. Perhaps you'd prefer to talk to them through the intercom?

Why didn't you tell me about that before? Hedge constrained himself. Valuable time wasting.

Didn't cross my mind. Actually old chap let's face it - they're resentful - you wouldn't get much out of them - try if you like the intercom - they'll blank you! Or caper face pulling yelling vile insults or cajoling why don't you come in and say hello and we'll tell you everything. That sort of thing.

But if you go in direct - face to face - you'll gain their respect. There's a chance they may open up. I've psychologically profiled that bunch.

Have they gone backwards then would you say? As human beings? Since the disaster?

Can you know the depths of being human, Inspector? You can find it here. With the incurables. Look I wouldn't put you through this if I didn't think it was the only way. So there - it's not too late to draw back and no man can call you a coward for doing so.

Hedge frowned. Decision time. But the decision had been made years ago when he put on a uniform of blue and gained an identity that had been eluding him.

I'm going in and that's that. I've had enough mucking about.

Belcher brought the inspector a white coat and a surgical mask and helped him to don same. Hedge hated him. Revenge. Must wait. Like to catch him in a loo sometime doing a bit of cottaging. The law still came down hard on that. Entrapment. You're a good looking young cop, Michael, now you get down that toilet and flash it about a bit. Like fishing. Big catch in Shepherds Bush near the BBC. Did he feel sorry for them? Them. Them. Why was it always them? Not us. No, you needed to put clear water between them and us, sisters under the skin...

This gown and mask are only for your morale dear, murmured Belcher. . Don't imagine they will offer you any protection at all at all.

I heard that, Nurse. Fettle sharply retorted. Do not demoralise the inspector.

Why not? What's he ever done for me?

The facts will speak loudly enough, Nurse.

They'll have speak loudly if he's in a lead lined casket.

Gallows humour! I told you about that, Inspector. Hardly the time and place, Nurse Belcher. We have a visitor. Show some discretion.

Hedge said, That's alright. I like a laugh as well as the next man.

There won't be anyone else after you don't worry, said Belcher.

Just then a tantrum blew up in the ward. Was it much? As Hedge stepped towards the door Morgan threw himself at the observation window and pounded it with his fists. Then he started picking up vases and objects and threw them at the window. They bounced off harmlessly enough - made of some pliant compound. A silent show.

Hold it, said Fettle, will he go for the big stuff - stand by Belcher.

CS5 sir.

The others inside the ward watched Morgan - desperate - tiring - then Fletcher got out of bed - sort of quiet.

Watch out - stand by - Fletch is up - stand by...

Fettle grimly watched but seemed to enjoy it. Belcher with his jangling keys had unlocked the control valve for the chemical police agent aerosol spray. Hedge watched. Hello.

Hold it Belcher - he might not move, said Fettle.

Fletch yawned. Hedge watched, fascinated. Don't assume the man Fletcher was a lab assistant because of his colour. He could be a brilliant scientist. Why identify his occupation by his colour? Was he - Hedge - institutionally racist? He did not mean to be. Fletch was Black and Beautiful not White Trash like some he could mention. Morgan was doing a dance now - a war dance - OK - what - hardly moving Fletch had beckoned Morgan over to him and Christ - here goes - they lifted an iron bed up and threw it at the observation window. Hedge ducked.

Right, shouted Fettle. Let 'em have it!

The bed bounced off the window silently. God knows what din was going on the other side - for now they seemed to be having their fun. A riot. Belcher leered and turned on the gas - and soon - soon - they slowed and collapsed - staggered - and collapsed. It was over.

Blast, said Fettle. Sorry - oh why - that's enough Belcher - don't overdo it. Well old chap... And he took Hedge's arm. We aren't having much luck are we? That's another twenty-four hours down the drain - clearance - sorry.

Hedge resigned took off his gown - surgical mark one - right choked he was - and walked off up the corridor forgetting to remove the surgical mask.

Perhaps you'd care for the communion service in the morning, called out Fettle. Harvest Festival - we try and keep life going on as normal - the normal you are familiar with - while we're waiting for these nits to die off! Sorry, I can do professional concern - never mind- what a trouble! What a disappointment. The party's over for today!

Hedge muttered something and realised that he was still wearing the surgical mask. He tore it off in disgust. Another night with those kidney bowls.

CHAPTER XXIII

Inspector Hedge was in his kidney shaped room - so it seemed to him - reading some old Woman magazine. Not a magazine for old women - for witches and curses and ever-filled purses - rather advice on unhappy relationships but could he label Doris as unfaithful - surely she had not inflated herself and floated away...

Whether it was night or day he could not tell, no window beckoned him. He had his watch if it had not been tampered with and anyway it was a twelve hour period.

He was choked and lay on the bed reading the agony column. Women seemed to have a lot more could go wrong with them than men and they had a lot of emotions that a policeman did not have. Of course there were policewomen of the non-Inflatable variety and they had emotions - stuff that your average cop did not - no mate better to put your gun in your mouth and pull the trigger.

Belcher entered without knocking bearing a tray which he placed on the bedside cabinet.

Supper.

Rat. Oh you fink. Bet you write half these letters about women's monthly times. It was to do with the moon eh? Well his own emotions were tidal as far as he knew - face that - nothing to be ashamed of - that did not make him gay as in Gay Parade! My God what would they think of next? Inspector Hedge you are homophobic. The law is changing darling. Hold hard - I am upholding as is the law against all comers. And shall we say against your own inclination?

Belcher sat on the bed. If I was hard on you, Inspector, I'm sorry. I don't know why you got mixed up in this? I really don't a nice man like you being thrown to the wolves it is. I'll just sit here a minute if you don't mind - always on the go - Belcher do this Belcher do that! Go here go there! Fetch this fetch that! Empty that bedpan! I'm running a one man show here I tell you...

You don't have to talk. Sit there if you like nurse.

They sat, him in the easy chair, her - was it her - on the bed and the silence deepened between them and for a moment held its own forgiveness. Pity me not sweet sir, that shall not be. What previous life tells me when and where? What? What? Did I play a sweet maid so usurped by violent man? And betrayed. Abandoned by a soldier with a babe to come. All forgotten now a boy in blue - with a truncheon and a shield and a helmet and a horse and beating down on rioters - this new life - what say you now my pretty maid? For I am reinstated and don't go for this Gay thing. I'm on the prancing horse accompanying the parade! Proud Not To Be Gay...

Belcher sensed how quickly changed the mood. He stood up, looked at Hedge as if to say something - changed his mind and left the room closing the door softly behind him. Hedge lifted the lid of his tray - not really interested - there was a great whack of corned beef - a few boiled spuds - a cooked tomato - later he'd have a prowl round - see what he could find - might find a decent bit of grub somewhere they must have a kitchen. The wall panel slid open and Shirley stepped through.

How did you get here?

Gawd knows - I found a vent like - in this ole tree.

See anything else on your travels?

I'm starving.

Dig in matey.

Shirley took the knife and carved a chunk of meat. There was a rattle as a bullet dropped from the meat onto the plate.

Hold it - for God sake don't eat that - it might be Ernie.

Wot?

A clue at last. A bullet. Had the process begun?

For Gawd sake put that bloody meat down - its's contaminated likely.

Shirley went to eat it and Hedge struck the fork away from her mouth.

Are you a ruddy cannibal?

So Ernie had been shot - canned - was that it - and a thoughtful tin provided from the consignment for good old Inspector Hedge - the first attempt on his life this thousand times corrupted meat - he'd been expecting it - but there was the bullet - chance in a thousand - this must have killed Ernie. He carefully picked up the bullet in a serviette.

This a rattling good yarn, he said. It's got to lead somewhere. Go on you can eat the tomato...

CHAPTER XXIII

Inspector Hedge and Shirley crawled through the undergrowth. He knew she was a girl - or he strongly suspected it - had he not himself - a young woman then - disguised as a soldier chased his lover to France and on the plains of Waterloo given birth midst the battle? Was it the medication talking and to whom? What interested him about her - girly Shirley come on you don't fool me - was which side was she on? You don't find a vent like that in a tree by chance and find your way into my room...

What were those early plans he had for her? He had thought of her as a boy worthy of adoption and to become a partner in a detective agency once he had retired - all gone now - candy floss. What were these intentions? All comes to naught. He had a job to do and trusted nobody - you could not afford to get involved with someone you met on a case - classic symptom - film script stuff - whoever she was - it was a bit hurtful - let it hurt, Inspector. Yes you did have feelings. My my! My Agony Aunt! But yes he had a job to do. His job. His life in danger. That's how he knew he had a life because it was in danger. And the Nation could be in danger. That's how he knew he was British...

Who had killed Ernie?

Had he been dead when he first saw him?

Yes - probably - awaiting disposal - transportation - oh yes it was all clear to him now - some people forgot he had five O levels - the doctors had killed Ernie - kill the meat - fresh - to keep the bug alive - Code Name Green Swan - and ship it out to our allies - what a rotten plan - what a way to treat a fellow creature - so they only had two weeks to live - that did not make them carcasses - to be used in the Cold War? What?

War touched the generations of his family. Hot war. Cold War. She - that was him then her at the Battle of Waterloo who had given birth in a square as the fighting raged - the French cavalry could not break that square as they rallied and charged again and again but the Redcoats held and horses cried in death pains as the baby cried into life and the mother I was died of exhaustion - how sorry was the soldier lad then to have abandoned his sweetheart.

Wot, said Shirley.

One day, said Hedge, a tale to tell - I'm not rubbish you know. Don't you care about history?

No I'm modern, said Shirley.

None of us is modern lad. Us is all a mix of a thousand stories. Don't you get carried away thinking of yourself as modern. Hedge took out his dental plate. See these front teeth.

Wot about 'em?

Knocked out they was in Trafalgar Square. Anti-nuclear demo it was lad.

That ain't history, said Shirley. having your teeth knocked out in a demo.

By a pole it was.

Who?

No not a Pole. Polish.

Polish?

By a pole from a banner.

Where'd he come from?

You play ignorant. What do you know? You can listen to me and learn something. You are ignorant - you don't have to play ignorant.

Don't rub it in.

He put his teeth back in. It's all history, he said. Many lives. In one, lad. Though he knew for near certain he was talking to a lass. What's the difference? She was smart - smart enough - and company for him and maybe he could keep his dream alive of the detective agency with her.

He could not bear to be crushed again, Inspector Hedge. It wasn't the having you teeth knocked out in a demo - it was them laughing at him behind his back at the Yard - figure of fun - yet he would show them - bring home the bacon.

Lad, listen. He sang, I'll list for a soldier and follow my love!

That was my story, he said. The favourite! As a young lass myself - the Battle of Waterloo. See the mother died - that was me I'm sure - haemorrhaging blood lad that mingled with the blood of the dying soldiers. And what happened to that fair soldier boy - he took his babe and bid farewell to his dying sweetheart...

Wot was you, said Shirley.

Right. And he hid the babe - the baby like - in a hedge till later - till after the battle but he was killed too and it was a Frenchy who came upon the mewling infant in the hedge and took it - and called it Jack Hedge see?

How did he know the baby was British?

Cos it was wrapped in a Union Jack.

Oh. Well how did he know the English word for hedge?

That's my name see? You're smart as paint 'ain't you? It's been handed down, said the inspector tinged with pride.

But you should've been called Jack Bocage cos that's the French name for hedge.

So you're not so bloody ignorant are you? And I weren't the baby I was the mother. But the name has been handed down through generations until I appeared again.

This time as a Police Inspector, said Shirley.

I probably met you before as well , he said. It can happen through time.

Which of course does not exist looked through other eyes.

Is you a philosopher or a copper?

Ever was my problem lad. One can be both. Now you hang on here, I'll scout ahead - in the bocage.

Truth to tell he was glad to get away from the lad or lassie - why had he unburdened himself to her - like that - blurting out his family history like a madman 'cos who would believe him he had been at Waterloo with the Duke of Wellington - that didn't go down well back at the Yard - had to keep schtum there keep your lip fastened - just tell jokes sort of thing - have you heard this one? Filthy jokes that he found boring anyway so they thought he was stand-offish - always reading head in a book him - well screw them he was on a case of the most delicate nature - he had been chosen not them. But of course there was PC Mathew yes now he was an intelligent chap good company he could share with him - until his funeral like. A self-inflicted wound poor Brian. One good friend not to be denied. Next subject! The Cold War yes - war is commerce at an-other stage - who said that? Not the sort of thing he would say - a Police Inspector a member of the Constabulary - he'd always been a bit bolshy and read stuff like Brian. Talking books they did. Forget Brian. Well he'd show them back at the Yard cos some weren't that bad but you had to run with the herd. Or get eaten by the lions. The point was - was there a point - it was immoral to kill someone to keep their meat fresh to ship it off somewhere - DEFENCE? Who defended Ernie? It was all beginning to tie up. They had played it too cool with him. Playing to his suspicions but he was ahead of their game. And now they wanted to kill him. That was a good sign - a sign that Inspector Hedge was on the case - he must watch out for himself from now on. Watch your back mate...

But why had they sent him on the case? Was it a matter of appearances? Putting up a show? Was it? A sacrificial victim he would do? Which side were the Yard on? To even ask... Inspector! Was he cracking? He served the Yard. Be upstanding for the Queen! What matter which side it was on. He had a job to do.

I wanna show yer the church, said Shirley.

She had disobeyed his orders to stay put and crawled through the undergrowth to be beside him. Anyway who was he to give her orders - come on Jack don't over-reach your remit - she was a factor in this case - hang on - there was the case and there were the bigger issues - like who was she? Really?

I'm on to you, he said.

Oh yeah.

Oh yeah. You watch it.

I would if I could find it, she said.

Cheek. Look I haven't got time for all this - you know - a talk sometime - this isn't the place.

Wot?

Wot? Yes I'm psychic - things I know - that get me laughed at so I stop right - stop saying it - too precious - casting pearls before swine so don't get me at it this is the wrong time.

Wot?

Wot? You was that soldier that got me pregnant and abandoned me I reckon - more than reckon - like it's a racing certainty - forget the other stories - cos I've seen you somewhere before - I feel you in my atmosphere I do that and you fit tight. It was you yes - Shirley - then our roles reversed as can happen in the sport and play of what is going on. So I found you on the battlefield didn't I and died giving birth to your brat and you died shortly after - a soldier lad blown to pieces for your country and here we are again up to our neck in it the garbage of history - us un-named besides the Great Generals - we has to mark our own graves - and who cares unless we tell our own story.

Oh yeah. Though it could be sung of course.

It was - you're right. I don't expect you to remember - all that living - all that dying - it's a gift or curse.

I wouldn't say you was wrong there.

Catching a moment of concern he kissed her and she did not resist for that kiss sealed their life and would go in no book about the new war - the Cold War. It was another meeting and they could name their children but the State would take them and feed them into the machine.

Whatever their names they would reduce them to numbers or cans labelled like Ernie.

She pushed him away. I'm only Nineteen.

And I was Eighteen once but that did not stop you did it?

He tried again.

But she was having no more of it - nor he for that matter - let the moment pass. He was on a case that was getting worse as he was getting better. Kissing her he felt alive and she was gone again into her role. She was more than Nineteen by the years and the rolling of the sun but that's what she was playing so let be...

You are to leave me alone, she said - no more of that right - what I was to you we'll never know through your addled brain so pay attention. You are to obey me at all times, right - I'm working for Sir Hilary Spong and so are you so less of the love life if you please. I'm wot? Wot? Wot? Do you get it?

Wot?

Hedge made to grab her again but she laid a hand upon his chest. No Jack it is the wrong chapter mate.

I don't care. I know what we were...

But he let her resist him with the lightest touch though he could see the sadness of it. He would not force himself upon her however many lifetimes it took.

Come to the church, she said - and not unkindly - there's something will interest you.

Gonna get married are we - publish the bans - Inspector Hedge's last case.

He let go of her and they made their way through the dusk to the chapel. Lights were on.

CHAPTER XXIV

Inside the chapel was a small pool of light by the altar. Shirley and Hedge watched from the dark at the back.

There - now, whispered Shirley as Fettle walked into the light and knelt in front of the altar. Then Belcher in white ruffle and surplice emerged from the dark shadows. He carried a bunch of twigs and began to belt Fettle.

What's this got to do with it? whispered Hedge. I'm not interested in their Harvest Festival rituals.

The lights on the altar slowly glowed up showing the beautiful arrangements of nature organised thus by the vicar. Atop all crowning the scene - the last to be illumined - was her The Inflatable One. Hedge might have guessed - felt deflated - punctured himself. He turned to Shirley - is this what you've brought me to see? He wanted to slap her face but would not violate her. What was this all about? That was his partner up there on the altar - a toy to their sick games.

Let's git, he hissed and strode out of the chapel. As Shirley followed the inspector the disturbance caused Fettle and Belcher to look back in furtive alarm.

Outside Hedge grabbed Shirley and shook her. That's my partner up there on the altar - don't you understand a professional relationship?

Wot? To that inflatable dummy?

Yes, that inflatable dummy - the one that doesn't answer back.

Why don't you grab her then?

What?

What was stopping yer?

Hedge didn't know what was stopping him. He let go of Shirley's shoulders. He said, I've got to let it play out.

I'm real, she said. Can't you take it?

He walked away into the night. He would find his way back into the clinic. His room. His thoughts. His bed. The kidney patterned curtains. His case - Oh yes don't forget that Inspector Hedge - a lot was hanging on that. His self-respect. What would it matter to him if he was sitting in the canteen on his own while they flicked bits of soggy bun at him - the others when they thought he wasn't looking - as long as he knew - as long as he knew he had solved it - Code Name Green Swan.

The problem was - as he lay upon his white enamelled iron cot in the darkness of his room - a small blue ceiling light producing shadows and comfort - the problem was that he was in his room where he felt relatively secure so was he becoming institutionalised? The chart on the end of his bed was still blank but how long would that last? Even he would appreciate something written on it so was he having an identity crisis? Like transforming into a patient? Mind first the facts would follow. Would his need for identity be the death of him? The death of identity be his life's chance? He knew it was a mistake though he did it to seek his identity in his work because when that went wobbly - when you were put out to grass, mate. Or had you put down out of kindness. Ways and means. But he still had a job. He still had a job and success did not mean that anyone back at the Yard apart from the Super would ever know that he had cracked it - brought home the bacon so to speak. He would still look a fool to most of 'em - the boys and girls in blue his comrades supposedly - well he'd feel better sitting there knowing what he had done what he had pulled off even if they didn't know. Brian would...

Ca va. Whatever will be will be as the song goes. His mind was wandering. He would follow it. Alice down the rabbit hole. Trouble was he was literate now that didn't go down well keep your mouth shut mate - play the fool yes The Scarlet Pimpernel - the fop - they laughed at him too taking a pinch of snuff on the back of his hand! Who was it now? Leslie Howard right... He was breathing... IN... Deep breath,.. Hold it... OUT... IN... Hold it... OUT...

Who was on who's side in this charade? A deadly game in which Code Name Green Swan could be an uncontrolled virus not just a weapon against the enemy but escaped a blight upon the land the new plague back to the Dark Ages with people jigging in the street ecstatic in death! Who were the enemy? Who were even now changing sides? Taking a position. Preparing for the consequences of the turmoil to come a sort of boiling up when groups of people would cohere by natural selection. Survival of the fittest. Meanwhile who was he, the Inspector, to take his orders from? There were no orders. There was no link he was on his own unless you counted that crazy girl saying you will obey me. Not as mutual marriage vows for sure. Till death us do part? Now that was possible. On this case. So far underground without a link a thread to spin into a cord and thus the rope to haul themselves out of the pit. The snake pit mate! It was all words in his head words words! And more words! He could not stop them. A loner. Not too too long on his own though if you please. He had signed on to work in the structure of the Force - One for All and

All for One - in theory that was not in the practice of the ambitious corridors of Scotland Yard where gossip could kill the unwary. Orders were becoming more impossible to obey - more and more absurd and profitless until loyalty and madness lay together unless you changed sides quickly to save yourself...

Which way to jump? .

The chit of a girl had the cheek to say you will obey me at all times as if she were linked to some hierarchy. Like plugged in. That's a comfort. Plugged in to insanities circuits more like a revolving brainstorm that was - now that could see them out of trouble! The Super yes he longed for an order from the Super something to put him straight. Get your man seemed quite sufficient for this case a simple murder was it? Concentrate on that and leave the big stuff to them Upstairs. Always someone Higher Up wasn't there? Gold braid out on special occasions like PC Brian Mathews funeral. Nice of them. Real emotion they had. Very handy. Stock in trade. Real tears blinked back behind the Ray-bans in the sunlight. The folded Union Jack handed to the widow...

Was he falling down on the case? True you could apparently come and go within the parameters of the clinic. Behind the wire or through holes in the fence like a breeding rabbit but they were watching you...

He had found the tree and come down the vent on his own and almost wished he had brought her with him - he would like to interrogate her - teach her to get mixed up in this - she'd find out who was giving the orders alright - her place was at home doing the dishes. But those days were gone Inspector - get your pinafore on lend a hand - she'll be home presently and exhausted from a day at work and you mate yes YOU do the dishes! Do you want your dinner or shall I bung it in the waste disposal? Do as you like Jack I'm tired out I'm sorry I want to be more to you and I know you look forward to me getting home with the day's news and so on. And so on and on. Dear God it must stop somewhere...

Ernie. Who killed Ernie? Sleep.

CHAPTER XXV

The next morning when Inspector Hedge awoke - yet again - a dark suit was laid out for him. He recognised it as his own. Nothing surprised him now. OK they were in touch with the Yard and he wasn't. A change of clothes anyway. He had only brought a spare pair of socks and his weights God knows where they were probably returned to the Yard by now. He dressed carefully enjoying the feeling of clean clothes. He had showered before dressing life goes on. He noticed that there was a black armband stitched to his sleeve. Presumably he was going to a funeral. Shirley preyed on his mind - that's what he called her - he did not know her real name. Were names real? A rose by any other name would smell as sweet. He had dreamt about her during the night - they had been in Heaven together and Shirley had got into a terrible row with the Virgin Mary - hair pulling and all that because Shirley had said it wasn't fair on Joseph her getting pregnant the way she did but an angel had parted them and said let those without understanding get understanding...

Perhaps his big mistake was getting emotionally involved with his partner Inflatable Police Woman Doris. They had instructions for use of a PCW Mark I issued due to economies freeing up people for more paperwork - especially leaving her Doris in charge of the police car. She also had a camera attachment useful for hovering over and recording crime scenes. No one thought to warn of emotional attachment except for a few under the armpit jokes par for the course. They could not imagine anything sincere clumping around in their boots with their limited imaginations and stunted vocabularies. It was too late now - he was caught in his own storyline - his memories providing an ongoing narrative. He, Jack - hello Jack - could not let her down - Doris. He found a comb in his pocket with which to address his hair - slicking it back what was left of it. Doris might have recorded some interesting material. That's why he had left her in situ. In the chapel. Still not quite sure what triggered her tapes on. All very psychological! She had a mind of her own did Doris! That's a laugh. Well, let's make a day of it. He headed for the door.

He was walking in the hospital grounds with Doctor Fettle. There was to be a funeral,yes.

We've managed to decontaminate Ernie, said Fettle. So now we can do the decent thing and pay him our last respects.

It's a bit late for respect, grunted Inspector Hedge. And you cannot decontaminate dead meat so don't throw that one at me.

Nevertheless - and yes that was flimflam - my we are awake this morning, Inspector! Well done that man! Regardless, sir, there will be a service. Never too late to do a good thing.

Like putting enough lifeboats on the Titanic after it's sunk.

I appreciate your dour mood, Inspector. Things have not been easy here for you - or for any of us.

And certainly not for Ernie, Doctor. Someone killed him. You want to make it look good. How come he didn't die in the plane crash you dreamt up?

He was a lab assistant for Heaven's sake that's why! He did not set out to the international conference. Satisfied?

I'm on a murder enquiry. There is no satisfaction without results. Nothing I have discovered persuades me otherwise than that Ernie was most foully despatched. Before his time - however limited - even be it a matter of weeks - or days - we all have a right to that span.

I'm glad you're making progress. And we are here to help and I am most sorry if there have been delays and frustrations.

On the contrary Doctor nothing has impeded my work. For those who would lay difficulties in my path incriminate themselves in what may be a bigger enquiry than was at first envisioned.

Oh dear, I hope not. Dear me no we all want to get back to normal as soon as possible at Howling Clinic. This was an unfortunate subcontracted Government job the Board decided... But there! It's done!

And you are on the Board, Doctor Fettle, I presume?

Razor sharp! Be careful you don't cut yourself, Inspector.

They were nearing the chapel.

One piece of good news, added Fettle brightly. The Incurables will be able to watch the service on closed circuit telly. Isn't that wonderful? It will have a calming effect. They need to be part of the closure of this matter.

Closure? The opposite is happening. It's opening up, said Hedge.

Well, yes I suppose. I meant that from our point of view it's better than using CS5 gas. Though it does give us an opportunity to experiment with the product. Here we are! After you, Inspector, please...

They entered the chapel.

Someone was playing the organ seeking the lost chord. In the choir stalls sat Belcher done up in his gear cassock surplice ruffle my a girl does get around! He was seated next to several young people similarly attired - my God the fox was in the henhouse - he would watch Belcher more than ever he would watch Belcher. No sign of Doris on the altar - where had she got to? At the opposite end of the choir stall to Belcher was seated Shirley.

Doris and Shirley? Wasn't he a card? He had women trouble alright. The thought lifted his spirits...

The choir burst into song and sweetly they sang. Belcher had a high contralto voice of utter purity as if the Gods had blessed him deliberately with a gift with which he could gain entrance to innocent hearts and minds. You watch it Belcher. What was Shirley doing in with that lot? She looked nice - wholesome that girl - no-one'd think she had been tugging the hair of the Virgin Mary! A dream. Get thee understanding.

Inspector Hedge joined in the singing meanwhile surveying the scene. A lot of strangers in today - open house - make it look good. A Ministry of Defence special. Good cover. You don't fool me mate. Few patients sprinkled around - laugh - there was old Mr Plerns standing at the back - bolt upright in his wheelchair singing away. Staff. Faces. Vaguely somebody. Could be extras bussed in. He looked again at Shirley. She smiled beatifically then gave him a wink. Hello! Watch it unfold he tried to convey...

The hymn finished and the music became sombre. Here came the principal mourners he'd know them a mile off some of those doctor bastards. They were bearing the coffin on their shoulders. Watch out chaps! As they passed by the end of the pew where he had placed himself Hedge threw the banana skin in their path. It was the banana that had been given to him by the Super. Not a trick missed he'd eaten the banana which was Phase One. Now came the dangerous bit. The first mourner passed alright his feet missing the banana skin and for a moment Hedge feared they'd all miss it and then Hallelujah the last mourner of the clown troop passed and whoops! Stagger! Sway! Yes, no, hold on...

The moment poised in slow motion - the gathering silence - the sheer kinetic energy of the avalanche and...

OHHH LOVELY JOB!!!

CRASHING TO THE FLOOR THE COFFIN CAME ON ITS SIDE THE LID FLYING OFF...

And as the inspector suspected dozens of tins of corned beef scattered out from the coffin over the aisle...

The congregation aghast! Bemused! Agog! Turning! Churning! The storm whipping up...

Fettle furious fuming!

Belcher blowing wind!

The vicar flapping reaching for the Cross of Christ to hurry down the aisle and sanctify what could be saved!

And in the choir stall Shirley on her toes to catch the drama, laughing fit to bust!

Jack had scored today. She guessed right. Time to go Inspector Hedge. None But The Brave...

CHAPTER XXVI

Inspector Hedge sat in his room and considered. Well that should get 'em going. That should hit the Monday headlines! But it would not - no - patients and staff signed up to the Official Secrets Act - well staff anyway and patients what was to become of them - a cover for the mischievous operation going on underground - The Incurables - Code Name Green Swan. The patients were oblivious not only to the drama going on beneath their feet but of most other things except their own fantasies. And the point was he Inspector Hedge was also a patient so what might he be fantasising? On the medical chart at the bottom of his bed while he was away someone had written in bold words,

POSSIBLE PARANOID SCHIZOPHRENIA.

Was this some sort of joke?

More like a deliberate ploy to unsettle him?

To un-nerve him?

They - whoever THEY were - were worried because he was on the case - Inspector Hedge yes watch out - and he was - Mark it! - closing in and they knew it even if he was not aware of the progress he was making when people started reacting you know you were touching sensitive spots! And maybe the banana skin slipped into the aisle had been seen reported considered and with due consternation and haste this was their response...

FORGET THE MEDICAL CHART! He wasn't falling for that one, mate!

He was not paranoid schizophrenic ... though... though... though to be fair if he was how would he know?

Inspector Hedge paced up and down in his room which was not a lot of pacing. As to the church congregation most of them looked like second rate actors on a daily rate. In which could be absorbed such as MI5. And riffraff from the corridors of power being given useful employment instead of hovering round the tea trolley all day gossiping about the Cold War. And don't tell me the Russians weren't in? There were a few blue-chinned Goons sprinkled around. None of them at the funeral service were relatives of the supposedly deceased or missing believed killed scientists. Excepting possibly relatives of Ernie. Did Ernie have relatives? Good question. He didn't look the type to have relatives. He looked more like a mutant - a one-off no relations no mother - a manufactured item that's how he looked to Inspector Hedge viewed through the perspex window of the casket in the morgue. Now chopped and minced Ernie. Tinned Ernie. Who needs a mother to grieve a tin of meat? Good point...

He was dealing with a murder but behind it were the ravages of a biological warfare experiment gone horribly wrong and yet they - THEM - they were still trying to salvage research from it and to profit from it by selling information and product to the Yanks. They were trying to save their jobs weren't they? They were trying to save their necks while Britain stood on the brink of disaster. What was genuine Ernie in the consignment of falsely labelled corned beef? Chopped up ground up Ernie? Had the vicar - a powerful man in a perverted way - demanded a sanctification of Ernie's remains or was the vicar more than he seemed - the leader of a cult - thrashing Fettle with the twigs or deputising his acolyte Belcher to do the job? Who was the Grand Master round here? Of the Black Arts?

Wisdom is the principal thing; therefore get wisdom: and with all thy getting get understanding.

Where did these words come from? His granny who always carried round a bible - his granny who always cared for him and prayed for him - Gran - good old Gran - you couldn't take her seriously as she waddled around her bible clasped between her hands - always in black she was like an ancient peasant - but kind she was and smiling and laughing too! Ah well she had religion - not his cup of tea - yet her words she spoke to him now...

And with all thy getting get understanding.

He wanted to understand this case. But did he have a life beyond it? Case after case - prying all the time into other people's lives that what it was - with all thy getting Get A Life, Inspector - get understanding - understand you were going down the tubes son - get a grip - let go - what?

Nurse Belcher came in - without knocking - with the sweetest of smiles and several letters.

Your mail, sir! She curtsied and left.

Hedge pounced upon the letters. My God from the Yard - Yes - No c/o the Yard from his mother. The Super had posted on a batch of letters from his mother without even a covering note. So in touch but a million miles away. He knew her writing. Always care of his Super because he had broken off correspondence with her - broken off contact - but she had found a way and at the same time compromised him with the Super - with the Super yes who must be laughing at him having a mother sending letters to her son care of Scotland Yard. Not hate mail you understand - no - but neurotic whinging clawing him back to the womb - he sent her money that he did - monthly. Cos her three husbands had died or gone away and he was sired of one of them not a thing to talk about too much violence in the household when he was a kid and how could he protect her? Mum - he'd found a way to brain the guy another dad he was drunken and violent Jack had hit him with a poker and near done for the bastard who had gone away to sea and then Mum blamed him her son, Cos she was left alone awhile and apparently he was not a bad man after all when he was sober. She'd found someone else.

He tore up the letters unopened. Till he left the Force he'd never be shot of her - damn shame really but he had trained himself the hard way. In all thy getting get a life.

Belcher was getting under his skin. He had wanted to leap up and accost him as he entered the room because it was different it was familiar it assumed what he was not ready to give and had always held back since... No, no reason - because - because...

Urges. Where did they come from? Was he possessed or just a closet homo?

This wouldn't do - these violent urges could be the making of him - a fascist pig as the demos called him - perhaps they knew him better than he knew himself. A fascist pig yes like the rest of them - reading didn't make him different - he - him - in his present reincarnation - had put on a uniform to steady the ship - to be somebody - not to have to think who he was or what he had to do - to enforce the law boy! But the law was changing and the gay parade was coming to town...

Did he need it thrashing out of him from Belcher? At the altar submitting - he could not bear the thought - surely being a fascist pig would save him - it went with the uniform didn't it? Why was he running away from it?

No, he would take the better path - the higher road - he would not give in to the forces of evil - he sent his mum an allowance didn't he - he was a good kid - he would write to her - one day - not now Mum - I can't read your letters now, I'm on a blooming case aren't I?

Sorry Mum. He picked up all the pieces of letter and placed them in his bag. Later. He could piece them together. He had other things to piece together now...

CHAPTER XXVII

Inspector Hedge could not keep out of the grounds. Well it was a nice day and he was not a bed case, not yet. He did not know what restrictions were upon him or if they - whoever they were - had orders to give him free rein. Out of his room he could walk in the nature and think. Or he could not think which would be more helpful. Listen to the bird song but where was it in this Silent Spring? What was happening? He spied Fettle spraying chemicals over the plant life. The doctor seemed to be enjoying his work. Probably a Sunday hobby of his. Probably got hold of some agent orange from his American friends in the Defence Department that they had left over from defoliating Vietnam. The doctor was wearing a mask - it had to be toxic that spray. The plants seemed to wilt as he pumped the mist onto them. He could have done it more easily from a helicopter, riding in on a chopper speakers blaring The Ride Of The Valkyries to defoliate Surrey. Good job.

Hedge noticed the vicar next - hang on - coming up the other side of the hedge that Fettle was spraying - the vicar with a shot gun and game bag my God nature was having a job to survive today between the two of them.

Wait - surely Doctor Fettle had seen him coming?

The doctor continued spraying and the vicar took a full whiff - waved his arms in the air as if in protest and staggered around in a reel and fell behind the hedge out of view. Was that an accident on this sunny afternoon? The doctor continued spraying along the hedge. Why? Was the vicar another manifestation of unwanted nature in the grounds of the clinic?

The inspector took refuge behind a tree. Had he just witnessed another murder? Had the vicar proved to be unmanageable? The vision came to Hedges inner eye of a scene he had witnessed as he was leaving the church the day before. Be-robed and vested the Vicar had stood in the foyer handing out tins of corned beef to a few of the congregation as they were being evacuated. There were some locals, Hedge sensed - a trusted few - zombies more like - they did not have to be robots - a stolid fealty to Queen and Country would suffice. It had to look like an Open Day and the Church was still decorated for Harvest Festival and it was customary to hand out local produce to the congregation...

Was the vicar deliberately giving out tins of contaminated Ernie?

It probably was corned beef - real tins of corned beef - they were symbolically placed into the coffin heaven knows why but not the real Ernie. Could be Mad Cow but that would be another story. If in his own mad improvisation of the moment - reckless or ignorant - the vicar had given to his parishioners tins of canned Ernie to take home there would be raids on the local district to reclaim the goods - dawn raids - people dragged out of bed - front doors smashed in! Where's your tin of corned beef then? It's contaminated you don't need to know any more. What's that dead cat lying in the corner?

Oh my God! Someone's opened the tin! Quarantine this house! Shoot the occupants out the back! Collect them in the covered lorry and take them to the lime pit...

All that might have been going on - could have already happened - he was in a time bubble and had to deduce his way out of it - for now but now he was witnessing another event. The doctor stopped spraying. He removed his mask and brought out a walkie-talkie and spoke into it. The inspector waited and as he expected it was Nurse Belcher that turned up accompanied by two orderlies pushing a stretcher trolley. They went behind the hedge and shortly afterwards appeared again pushing the trolley with the body - inert unconscious or departed spirit - of the vicar. They disappeared back into the building from which they had emerged. Fettle replaced his mask and resumed spraying...

Hedge had seen enough. He slipped back through the trees, found the one with the vent and entered down a runged ladder to a corridor - a corridor that led with any luck back to his room. But his luck took him elsewhere.

CHAPTER XXVIII

Inspector Hedge fell through the panel into the soft lighting and humming machinery of a room and regained his balance. He was in the morgue. The entombed casing which had held Ernie now contained another body. He approached it and peered through the Perspex window at the face - calm in repose but a bit stupid looking - even obstinate - obstinate in death - not enquiring, not interested, obviously keeping his own opinions - it still looked like Ernie.

It is Ernie, said a voice. Belcher had come up behind him. You'd better put this gown and mask on dear - regulations - I didn't make them.

Hedge let the queer nurse gown him up. This repellent attractive creature. It's all in my mind, his thoughts plagued him. I don't want to be homophobic. Each to his own. Yet what could he own of himself? That he needed to borrow a blue uniform and an identity?

You don't like me for who I am, do you dear? A pathetic pansy is that it? You don't know me darling. It took courage to come out in the army it did - last days of conscription love - and a few of us decided we would act gay to avoid going to a foreign country to meet interesting people and kill them - or them us dear, you get it? Not having that we weren't - being shipped out to Korea - so we started camping it up three of us we were - and got beat up a couple of times by our mates so called - and got put on kitchen fatigues and told our CO we'd love to meet some Chinese soldiers cos they were so butch - so they gave us a dishonourable discharge and I've stayed that way ever since - I suppose because it was my right of passage - and don't give me a vulgar answer dear.

Your ways are your business, son - I don't ask for explanations. It's still illegal.

What is? Being camp?

Careful son. They'll come down hard on yer. It's nothing personal. Let's leave it at that. What was in the tins of corned beef? Ernie ? Mad cow?

No, dear. Ernie.

Ernie?

They amputated a leg and minced it up into three tins labelled corned beef with special despatch numbers and put them in with a batch of corned beef that they had sent us...

They?

Them, dear, whoever they are. The Big Knobs. So it was all ready to go - this crate - but the vicar he kicked up a fuss and said to keep the peace with them in the incurable ward - the sickos - some sort of service must be arranged cos someone had died amongst them - and he must bless Ernie in the right setting - being the chapel of course - so as we couldn't move the rest of Ernie from the morgue - that was strictly prohibited - they put the tins of corned beef in the coffin, didn't they?

Including the three Ernie tins? Hedge was taking notes.

They said so but no. So the vicar - oh he's a crafty one - he knew they wouldn't - and he was determined to bless Ernie properly. And the vicar has powers beyond his station hereabouts.

What?

Because of his practices which he says ain't heretical but in line with the Ancient Church - chastising and all that carry-on dear - you know - we all join in the fun don't we?

Very bracing, said Hedge.

You should try it some time.

No thanks. The inspector manoeuvred himself round the other side of the capsule. Casket. Continue...

Well - where was I - oh yes the old vicar he knew they'd pulled a stroke and it would only be tins of corned beef and he wasn't going to bless them was he? Go to all that trouble? To bless tinned cow? And he has all the keys to this place whether they like it or not - the vicar yes - and he gets those tins of Ernie...

The three tins?

Yes that's right dear - out of the secure fridge in the secure unit - oh yes - placing three ordinary tins...

Of corned beef?

Well it wouldn't be tinned pears would it? Back in the fridge. And Ernie goes in the coffin.

Right, said Hedge. After the spillage at the service the vicar came down to the scene and started giving tins of corned beef to the congregation. Well it was Harvest Festival love. You give the produce away don't you?

Did that include Ernie?

He hoped so. You see Inspector - if you don't mind me being so descriptive - the vicar wished to lay a curse upon the land - that it shall be blighted and all shall be laid low you know that sort of thing - you know before the Second Coming - like a dreadful plague had to come before and he was the Chosen One to assist it - well whatever turns you on I say - it takes all sorts to make a world doesn't it?

Did the Authorities - do you happen to know...?

I know it all dear - try me.

Did they retrieve all the tins?

All except one.

Was it a tin of Ernie?

That I don't know. Sorry. So I'll have to keep you in suspense won't I?

My God, what a mess. The inspector put his notebook away. You didn't hear me say that. There is a plot to be unravelled here. I'd appreciate it if you keep what you've just told me to yourself.

Oh it's our little secret Inspector. Are you one of those queer bashers are you? Any opportunity is it? Down a dark alley?

No. Don't worry. You keep your side of the street Nurse Belcher and I'll keep mine. I realise you're as human as the rest of us.

That's very decent of you, Inspector.

It's not your fault.

What isn't?

Being like you are.

Who said it was a fault? The fault dear Brutus lies in our stars - and my stars darling are Rock Hudson and Burt Lancaster - bonar they are!

Doctor Fettle entered the morgue. Ah there you are Inspector! And I hope my nurse - the good Belcher - has been enabling you in your enquiries.

Was a bullet planted in my corned beef? Hedge directly asked the doctor.

That I would not know about. Bullets in your meat? Sounds like a long shot to me.

Let me put it another way Doctor, did you establish cause of death of Ernie?

Well no, we have been obstructed in carrying out an autopsy. In fact we have been directed not to touch the corpse - unless that is - unless for the specific reasons of the needs of Defence. Which rest beyond this clinic to determine.

Yet you or someone reported a murder.

Yes, well it seemed to me that Ernie had been asphyxiated.

How come?

He had a silk stocking knotted round his neck.

I see. Someone has removed it?

I don't know whom. Possibly someone who wanted to make up a pair. I would suggest that you retire to your room Inspector. By this evening the incurable ward will be available for your entrance - should you still be so madly inclined to do so.

Was the serum with which I was injected hatched from Ernie?

The doctor looked dubious. That is possible.

On whose instructions?

There you have it you see. Even I don't know that. All I know is that statistically I give you a seventy percent chance that the inoculation has taken.

Yesterday it was eighty percent.

Yes, well sadly one of the laboratory rabbits has died since then. Do mull it over Inspector. After all nothing is decided until you actually enter the decontamination chamber.

CHAPTER XXIX

Inspector Hedge entered his room by the door for a change - not falling through a panel from the secret passage. On his bed asleep lay Shirley - a young woman for sure - what was she doing here? What were any of us doing here? Anywhere. He slumped into the easy chair and stared at the kidney curtains. She was a reporter was that it? A new thought. You are to obey me at all times I am working for Sir Hilary Spong - she had said that - but then people say all sorts of things - things that come into their head like he did - improvising - and meanwhile life was happening - the gift of speech - the disguise of nature - the plumage of mankind - speech - to attract to bemuse to ensnare - he'd had enough of it. Rest. She might be who she said she was...

He was doing his job - he had asked questions - to attract to bemuse to ensnare. And they had answered in a similar vein - to attract to bemuse to ensnare. It was a game and the stakes were high - perhaps the desolation of the countryside - not seen since the Middle Ages - the Plague -

creeping into the towns started by a tin of corned beef - corned Ernie. A rogue tin. The one that got away - to fulfil the prophecies of a mad vicar.

Wake up, he said.

Oh hello. She blinked and smiled - lovely for a moment and his heart leapt. Could he rescue something for himself from the desolation to come? But no he would be true to his vows - well his allegiance - and be worthy to wear the uniform.

What are you thinking she asked him and sat up.

I know who you were he said. And who I was - previously like - on the plains of Waterloo. He frowned and went on... You made recompense to me for the sake of love and died as a soldier boy - so you see I bear you no ill-will.

That's nice she said. Taa for that.

Which brings us to today. Who are you?

If I told you would you believe me?

Try me.

I'm working for MI5. Her voice had changed. Where was the disgruntled kid? Like - what?

Like what? She said and laughed. I had to get in as a patient she said. And looked at him a moment. Can you take the truth?

Just give me the facts Ma'am said Hedge parodying an American TV show.

The facts aren't what they seem. Some of your experiences recently have been hallucinatory.

How would I know when they'd stopped? asked Hedge. I am on the case - now you tell me half of it is hallucination so how am I going to sort out the evidence?

With my help. Follow the bread crumbs out of the forest.

Hansel and Gretel? I've already used that imagery and I only got as far as the cottage.

The trouble did not start there said Shirley. It started in the biological warfare unit - practising evil they succumbed to it.

Black magic said Inspector Hedge. I see. Well I have evidence of that. Now listen here - you - whoever you are...

Joyce.

Joyce is it? Not a way-some lad - or lass - but now a fully fledged member of MI5 is that it? Very well I can get my head round that but should I? Because you are weaving words - a spell - give me some evidence.

Code Name Green Swan she said.

Did you pluck that from my subconscious? Mind reading are you?

I must go Jack.

What is your status here now? You've been turfed out once. Or was that a pantomime staged for my benefit?

I am a day patient. A Just For Today patient Jack. She knew his name and used it with familiarity which rang bells for him. Waterloo?

She went to the door. Beware - surprisingly they would bring back the magic arts of the Middle Ages if of any use to them - in Defence of the Realm think of that - all things are being studied scientifically - but those magic arts have their own agenda Jack. Take care - this is an unwholesome stew.

She blew him a kiss and was gone.

So Shirley had disappeared in a maze of words and come was Joyce the smart chick an MI5 agent battling an errant strain of witchcraft entered into the body politic - in the name of Defence was that it? What were we defending? And he was now to sort out his experiences as to hallucinatory or real as if he did not have enough to deal with.

He lay down upon the bed and felt the contours of her body. Oh Joyce or Shirley or the far gone Margaret who had marched to the sound of the soldiers' drum and given birth in the blood soaked square at Waterloo -

her own blood added as new birth came in the heat of battle and she had died but that was him and she was Jack the soldier boy then and here we are again. She knew naught of that - he had insight had Jack - had it since a nipper and learnt to hide it from mockery - what next Jack? He fell asleep and the cannon roared and the shouts of the French cavalry once more assailed his ears and the flash of steel and it's ringing and more cries and shouts and a baby mewling. To a deeper sleep the inspector went where he was a lad without a daddy and feeling lost and that he could never have what the other boys had - and girls too - and he would cry and resolve that his true dad was out there somewhere and he would leave home and find him which he had done several times - a runaway and recognised a stranger who denied him...

Yet deeper he slept. He was in a ruined city the buildings like broken teeth gaping and no-one else was about and it seemed to him it would be safer to find some habitable dwellings and some street life but the further he ventured the more desolate it became this city of looming ruins and old universities where now no word remained.

CHAPTER XXX

The metal shutter was down - closed over the observation window to the incurable ward.

Why is that? Asked the inspector. Why don't you keep the incurable patients under constant observation?

We found it was too depressing for our staff, answered Doctor Fettle. And the patients - they do not like to be constantly observed like goldfish in a bowl. Besides which we have them under scrutiny enough on closed circuit TV.

Who witnessed the murder? Inspector Hedge enquired.

No-one. No-one outside the ward that is - unfortunately - or you would have a clear-cut case, Inspector.

But you have the tapes - the video tapes for the period the murder took place?

Unfortunately wiped.

On whose orders?

Economy drive. They are not kept more than two weeks then recycled.

But the murder took place within the last few days.

So it did.

Well?

The tapes were still wiped, I'm afraid to report.

Why?

Because of the murder I presume. Why else? A most unusual procedure. We were instructed to send the tapes covering that period to - well I don't know where? A courier came on a motorbike and collected them.

But they were already wiped?

Yes - true. I suppose - to hazard a guess it was an inside job.

Not inside the ward?

No, inside the hospital administration.

Who looked after the tapes?

The vicar.

What has he got to do with such matters?

Ask me another one. It was the vicar's responsibility to change the tapes fortnightly and to wipe them. But immediately after the murder he came - on scene so to speak - and changed the tapes.

But why would the Vicar - who is concerned with spiritual matters and the comfort of the patients be entrusted with that task?

I've already told you I don't know. There was a reorganisation about six months ago - by security - the vicar was put in place - tasked with caring for the tapes.

Didn't you think that was strange?

I thought the whole affair was strange, Inspector. The least likely people taking authority. Or being given it. By whom you ask? The next question, Inspector. You have recovered fully your faculties I notice. Not the fevered wreck who arrived here for emergency treatment.

I did not come here to be treated. I have come here on a case. A murder enquiry.

A beneficial coincidence my dear Inspector. I cannot answer more questions at the moment. Some time later perhaps.

Hang on - would you happen to know the whereabouts of the vicar?

I do have a jolly good idea where you will find him, yes.

Fettle pushed a button and the shutter silently slid up. There spread against the observation window like a fly was the vicar.

He'll get used to being in there, said Fettle. I'm afraid they bit him.

Hedge knew that the last time he had seen the vicar he had been gassed by a toxic spray pumped over him in the garden by the doctor - then what?

Chucked into the incurable ward? To fend for himself?

Likely injected by Code Name Green Swan since he had become so dangerous - erratic was the word - was this a punishment for handing out tins of minced Ernie? Was the vicar to pay the ultimate price for his prophesy?

Hedge stared through the observation window as the other patients unstuck the vicar from the window and led him to a bed. They lay him down.

I will lay me down and die. A snatch from Maxwelton's Braes are Bonnie - where early fa's the dew...

His mother used to sing it - Hedge - Jack as a boy - and now look where he was - on the case, Mum.

I'm going in there, he said.

Surely not, Inspector. We've lost one good man - I'm pretty sure of that - his faith won't save him this time. I cannot recommend that you enter the incurable ward - for any reason whatsoever - and certainly not for the fatuous - excuse me yes fatuous - reason of following a murder enquiry when all the suspects are already sentenced to death. How many days? Two weeks at the most I give them - and the vicar will surely follow. I have his blood results. What more do I have to say to persuade you? Inspector it's as good as suicide to enter that ward.

You gave me a seventy percent chance of avoiding infection?

I'm afraid it's fifty percent now. Two more lab rabbits have died - unfortunately.

What about the rest of the rabbits?

All thriving. Bouncing bunnies. The worst for them is over.

Then I'm a bouncing bunny. Belcher - Nurse Belcher - a gown if you please.

Belcher fetched a gown from a cupboard. Don't be a mad fool Jack, he whispered.

How do you know my name?

Medical records. National Health Number, what else? You've made friends here Jack - don't leave us please.

What's this? A tear? A performance eh?

Belcher tied the green gown in a bow at the side and handed the inspector a mask.

I'll be praying for you.

Ok get out of my body space will you? Hedge didn't know whether to smack him or give him a big kiss.

Doctor Fettle who had been writing up notes came back to them. I need you to sign this, Inspector. It's a piece of paper that exonerates the clinic from all responsibility for this action and states that you have been warned of the possible consequences of entering the incurable ward and that you do so of your own free will.

Inspector Hedge signed the paper.

And could you write your next of kin where it is indicated.

Oh it 's his mother! Cried out Belcher, cramming closer to have a look. A mother's prayers can save her son! Thank Gawd!

Hedge could feel the nurse's hot breath on his neck as he whispered again, don't go through with it luv - I'll come to your room tonight - I can tell you a lot - everything - trust me.

For a moment the decision Hedge had made to go into the ward went back in the mix - but could he trust Belcher - did he really want that big queery faggot coming to his room in the middle of the night? Hedge was sweating - what was he frightened of? What was he running from? Belcher in the night - all enveloping Belcher - or the odds of surviving in the incurable ward?

Well we're all signed off, said the doctor breezily. All shipshape and Bristol fashion! If you're still of the same mind that is, Inspector.

Let's go.

Follow me, said the matronly nurse Belcher - all emotion tucked away - a job to do. I shall accompany you into the decontamination chamber.

Fettle said, We have to ensure that you take no viruses into the ward - strange as that may seem.

The doctor twisted and spun the control on the door of the chamber which was rather like a bank vault and the masked up Nurse Belcher and Inspector Hedge entered the chamber. The door sighed to a tight fit behind them. Before them lay another door - the door into that immoral hell where a murder had been committed - was it merely boredom or a cry for attention? We'll find out soon enough, Hedge muttered under his breath.

What next? He asked Belcher.

The air is being changed. You can sit down if you like. Then you go through the next door - on your own.

Hedge was sweating - God was he sweating as cool air wafted into the chamber and maybe high oxygen content because he began to feel quite high himself.

Sorry to be a bother - if you could roll up your sleeve, Inspector - we need a routine blood sample - just place your arm in that cradle by the wall.

Hedge did as he was told and the cradle adjusted and a needle came out of the wall and entered his arm. He fainted.

CHAPTER XXXI

When he came to he was standing in the park - the underground park and there were the beautiful elephants grazing some way off - and there she was sitting under a sun umbrella and he was wearing his tropical gear the very same he had been wearing when he went in to see the Super at the Yard - so that added up. It was a beautiful day - sun - hot - a heat haze.

She was sipping a cool drink through a straw. He went up to her. Hello he said, is this a dream?

Nearby was the statue of Prince Albert still in a crate - the one he had seen unloaded from a lorry and lowered by a crane through a trap into the ground. It was all here - there were the Kangaroos hopping past. Not a bad case this to be on - he sat down beside her.

The trouble is, he said.

I know, she replied. We've got to see this through. They think that I'm an agent for a group Germs For Peace - that I came to them disguised as a patient - you know with mental problems.

You told me you worked for MI5, said Hedge.

That could still be true, she said.

How could he trust her? He had a clearer idea of her in a previous incarnation - this one was still foggy. Look - I don't know what to believe - I'm a simple cop.

If you believe that you'll believe anything - you're the most complicated pig I've come across. Yet still she was smiling - cool.

Actually, he said, I'd like to trust you but I can't - it would be prejudicial to this case - what do you suggest?

You can trust the real me, she said. But not the hallucinations.

How do I tell the difference?

Now that's your problem.

Sir Hilary Spong came by in a golf buggy and stopped for a yarn. Beautiful day! Lovely morning isn't it? Sort of morning you only get on the savannah. If you ask me they've done a tremendous job mocking up this park four levels beneath the surface. Now you may wonder why go to all that bother? It's down to funding - the grander the project the more likely you are to get it - think big that's the answer. Mind you the world needs lots of small solutions but the politicians don't do small that's why we need to decentralise - get down to earth or in this case under it - I say I've said something funny haha! Perhaps not. Never mind, I'm not going to let that spoil my day. Any questions? Speak up or forever hold your peace!

Sir Hilary, you are a specialist...

In my own field, Inspector, yes.

How do I tell the difference between hallucination and reality?

It's got that bad has it? Haha. When you get out of here do come and see me in Harley Street. Here's my card - be sure to call - I see a certain number of patients on the National Health and I can fit you in - tataa for now!

Sir Hilary Spong drove off. Hedge stared at the card then placed it in a pocket.

Joyce - Joyce is it?

Yes. She poured him a cordial from a jug into a tall glass and fished out bits of fruit to decorate it. Cheers.

Hedge took a straw from a container in the centre of the table and gratefully sucked up the cool drink.

Listen Jack, the only way we could get in here was not as pretend patients but as real patients or the doctors would have seen through us.

I've not come here as a patient, Shirley - sorry, Joyce - I have been sent here by my Superintendent - I have all the credentials - they were expecting me - someone reported a murder.

Please yourself, darling.

Though - OK the Super did say set a sicko to catch a sicko - and they drugged me after I got here on the pretence that they were inoculating me against...

Code Name Green Swan, she said. Does it matter how you got here, Jack? Me too - I was heading for a nervous breakdown or - put it another way - I was in trauma when they came to me - the Firm - to my bedside and asked me to work for them.

They came to you in mental hospital?

Where else would they get the loon they needed? I was checked out. Bright. Intelligent. Oxford. But they needed to recruit me while I was still disturbed shall we say? Then they could get me transferred here - MI5 - because it would not only look real it was for real. So I agreed and they genned me up and here we are. You're reinforcements, Jack. How's your drink?

It's doing the job. And Sir Hilary Spong?

He's been on the inside a long time. We've been waiting for this. We knew - well they knew - that the Defence establishment were getting in too deep - that it would blow up in their faces one day - the dark forces they were dabbling with. Experimenting. That's what scientists do.

There was an experiment?

Of course, yes. And the opportunity the disaster would give to alien powers.

Alien? Hedge was alert.

Well unworldly. It's hard to describe them accurately because we don't know who they are... they are... they are...

You're fading out on me. Hedge was hearing her on echo - Joyce was coming in and out of focus - her voice becoming distorted and another voice superimposing itself...

Wake up - wake up old chap. It was Doctor Fettle shaking his shoulder.

I have some good news for you. Your Superintendent intends to visit you as soon as he can get away.

Inspector Hedge was in his room with the kidney curtains, lying on his bed. Doctor Fettle sat beside him.

And more good news, Inspector - hello? Are you with me?

Yes...

I'm sure you are well enough to take your meals with the other patients. No more hiding away in your room. You must mix with the others - get out and about. And partake of the occupational therapy facilities which are lavish or more than adequate here. Do you like table tennis? Or gym cycling? It's not all basket making! Or sickos eating bits of the sky from the jigsaw puzzles.

Hedge was not sure - grappling with what he was hearing - was he now in deep cover? He would go along with it - it was a stratum of consciousness which he would mine for information. Thank you Doctor. He blinked and played docile.

Lunch in half an hour then.

CHAPTER XXXII

Inspector Hedge entered the dining room. Here were the patients assembled lining up with trays to help themselves - about twenty of them. He took a tray and served himself and looked for a strategic place to sit. There she was - slouched over a table in the corner - as much out of the way as she could be without hiding behind the curtains. He crossed the dining room to her.

Do you mind if I join you?

Wot?

If I sit here? Is it alright?

Alright? What's alright?

Me. Here. Sitting.

Why would you want to do that cock? Fancy me do yer? Heard I'm a nympho have yer? Heard that? Want a shag do you?

No, just a bit of conversation.

I don't do conversation. I do shagging - so you can piss off mate.

Hedge put his tray firmly down opposite Shirley - she was more

Shirley today not the posh totty Joyce from Oxford. He laid into the food finding himself to be hungry. She stared at him.

Ain't you eaten in weeks?

I wouldn't know. I've been unconscious.

On a saline drip like?

Possibly. I wouldn't know.

Are your arms marked mate?

Could be. So…what's your name?

Margaret. Maggie like - but I ain't talking to you so you can fuck off.

Right. You haven't eaten much out of your tray have you?

Cos it's pig swill. For pigs mate - like you oink ! Oink !

How long have you been in here, asked Hedge, undisturbed by her manner.

Long enough to know a wanker when I see one. Listen mate - get it good - you ain't getting out of here mate until you been down under.

Down under where?

Under our feet mate - down under our feet - it's all going on - vivisection of mammals no less - and we go down there to get our memories wiped did you know that?

What have we got to forget then?

Wot? Listen mate they want you to remember what happened as a dream like? See them the enemy like - they won't know if they've surrendered or if they're winning or wot's going on - because this radar beam - like mate see - will scramble the inside of their 'eads - see? Are yer with me? Are yer? So when they wake up they won't know where they've been.

Like us, said Hedge.

Wot?

Same thing. They give us a real experience that we think is a hallucination and then a hallucination that we think is real.

Oh yeah.

168

They give the enemy the hallucination that all their cities are in ruins so they surrender and then later they find out we've occupied prime real estate - we don't have to rebuild the country!

You're still a wanker. That's why I won't tell you my secret.

What secret is that?

If I told you it wouldn't be a secret.

Yes it would - it would be our secret.

I'm a secret agent for Germs For Peace.

Are you sure that's not a cover?

What for?

Something deeper. The next level.

I don't know how many levels there are, she said and hid her face. Get away from me or I'll tell them you exposed yourself.

Where?

Here.

Right. I'm going - nice to meet you. Hedge stood up, He leant over the table and confided... At the next level you could be working for MI5.

Wot? Next level wot?

Down.

You're still a wanker.

He took his tray to the disposal area where he got rid of it and walked out of the dining room.

CHAPTER XXXIII

The inspector was walking in the clinic grounds with his visitor, the Superintendent. Hedge was wearing a loose fitting flapping in the gentle breeze hospital dressing gown. The Super was in civvies.

There are no microphones here, said Hedge. It's safe to talk. Except that we are listening which could present a problem.

The Super nodded. Well done , Hedge. You're in deep cover now.

I don't feel covered enough. Could you send in my pyjamas, sir?

Just give me a list Hedge - such things make it all the more convincing -

well done - well done! The chaps back at the Yard send their best for your speedy recovery!

I don't think I'm too popular back at the Yard.

Nonsense! You're revered! With your reputation I should cocoa!

Is that why they flick soggy bits of bun at me in the canteen?

You're too sensitive, Hedge! It's all in fun! All boys in blue together! What? When push comes to shove we close ranks! You're. a legend! We all love you! Did you get the Get Well card they sent you?

No. Hedge's eyes prickled with tears. Could they really care? Did he have to be ill before there was evidence of this? Pull yourself together Inspector - he took a deep breath exhaled slowly and said, I have to report that Inflatable Policewoman Doris Mark 1 is missing.

I see, said the Super. Any circumstances to report contributing to her disappearance?

Someone got hold of the kit and over-inflated Doris such that she became sky borne and then a certain Nurse Belcher out on a hunting trip shot her down. Or maybe the vicar, how do I know?

Hunting? In the grounds of the clinic? That doesn't sound right - are you sure?

Or back from hunting. I followed to where Doris went down - to make a retrieval of police property so to speak - but before I could get to her the Vicar grabbed her - the next I knew she was ornamenting his altar for the Harvest Festival where - I add - strange rites were performed in front of her out of hours.

My God what a sad story! Fortunately her recording device was running...

I must have inadvertently left it on, sir.

That was our luck. She transmitted some useful info before her battery went flat. Well Hedge that can happen on a case like this. I will get you a replacement kit - fear not - a Doris Mark 2 - with some improved features - you'll be glad to hear - because well you remember Sergeant Harris? He was caught in flagrante delicto with his Doris Mark 1 - damn fool - sort of thing if you're doing out on the job you make sure you don't get caught what? He lost a year's promotion over that.

Hedge frowned - not sure how to respond. So what is the point of improving her features sir - in a Mark 2 Doris?

Technically. Video camera.

Well - if you send me a Mark 2 Doris and Doris Mark 1 turns up again what will I do?

You'll be spoilt for choice won't you? Let's move on, Inspector - let's sit down on that bench - don't want you overdoing it.

Beside the path a bench. They sat upon it. There was a raspberry sound.

Did you do that?

No sir.

Another raspberry. They looked at each other - not sure - what?

Shirley or Maggie - what's in a name - emerged from the bushes behind them and sat on the bench.

Do you mind? We're having a private conversation, said the Super.

Don't mind me mate.

But I do mind.

It's a public bench mate. Like you don't own it.

Maggie or Shirley or Joyce whoever she anyway established she - whoever she was sat up the other end of the bench not budging.

She's a patient under deep cover, whispered Hedge. She's MI5.

Who said?

She said and she provided the code - Code Name Green Swan.

I see. The Super stared at the girl thoughtfully and said, Banana!

Fruitcake! She replied.

That all seems to be in order, said the Super. Now will you please go away.

If you don't like it here, mate, you can move on - not me - nobody's shoving me around mate.

She didn't answer the password properly, the Super said aside to Hedge but not particularly confidentially.

You said that all seems to be in order, replied Hedge.

Of course I did, Inspector. Because I don't say what I'm expected to say - or else anyone would be able to read me - got it? Now listen - that girl is potty. She's a mental inpatient here - you expect her to say things like she's in MI5 - don't you - course you do.

Are you talking about me, are yer? Are yer? I hear everything got bat ears I 'ave. Fancy a shag do yer? One up the front one up the back is it? All the same to me mate!

That's her cover, said Hedge. Being a Nympho. Don't pay any attention to that. She said - more or less and I might as well talk in front of her as we don't have much choice and I don't know when you'll be back.., She said that the biological warfare defence establishment has been infiltrated by the very forces that they are experimenting with.

Well she would say that, wouldn't she? She barmy. The Super turned to the girl - look if I give you some money will you go away?

You don't want a freebie then mate? Blow job no bother? You're not taking advantage. You might as well. Are you some sort of gent then are yer? Come in for a shag?

No, I'm interested how you came by the words Code Name Green Swan young lady?

Got 'em off the vicar dint I? Who got 'em off the incurables when he was in the ward.

You'd well to forget those words. The Super took out a five pound note and thrust it towards her. Here - you can go to the canteen and treat yourself.

She took the fiver and tucked it into her bra. OK you're a sport you are - you know that - you're good for one off the wrist any time guv! I never forget a face. And she was gone, skipping away up the path.

When she was well out of earshot the Super said, That's Margaret Emerson - she's a good woman believe me, the best MI5 have got -we're lucky she's on the case.

Hedge swallowed. I see yes - well moving on, Lionel, and I have taken that on board - since you are here visiting the sick and afflicted - and? Is your name Lionel? The meds they've pumped into me you understand....?

All in the line of duty, Jack. Jack bring your name right? Timely reminder. And Lionel will do nicely. Nobody's what they seem on this gig what - so who cares? Call me Lionel, yes, from now on I am Lionel. I like it!

There were shouts some way off. A group of people approaching.

What I want to know is - sir - Lionel - what is my mission statement? I mean other than to track down the killer of the murderer of Ernie - tinned Ernie as it turns out - I'm in for something bigger here, aren't I?

Your mission remains as described, Inspector. Although you are now able to understand that you are being used as a decoy - got it? So that they focus on you while Emerson does her work - because you see, Hedge - now that you can take it in - there are other elements to this investigation...

The noise was getting louder. Some sort of demo.

But, Inspector, should you break through on your mission - finding a weak point - you are to carry on, is that understood?

You mean my mission is not necessarily farcical?

Of course you are being used. We are all being used, Hedge, in various degrees.

With various pension schemes.

We like the bolshie in you Hedge. However neurotic your state there is the cool flame of rebellion - no - a flame of integrity that cannot be bought, Inspector...

VISITORS OUT ! VISITORS OUT !

It was a demo of patients - and before them falling back were a host of visitors in disarray. A banner proclaimed DON'T VISIT US - WE'LL VISIT YOU.

This is a madhouse, said Hedge.

You must join them Hedge, said the Super. Show solidarity. Throw me out - go on!

But...

No buts Hedge - lay hands upon me. Goodbye - don't try and contact me - we'll be in touch - find out what you can...

As the demo swamped them Hedge grabbed the Super and pushed him off the bench shouting, I didn't ask to see you! Leave us alone! Respect our privacy!

RESPECT OUR PRIVACY ! RESPECT OUR PRIVACY ! The chant was taken up. The broken ranks of visitors fled through the gates - grapes and various fruits and magazines and toiletries thrown after them. The gates swung shut electronically.

Hello - here come the riot squad! Nurses and orderlies wearing gas masks - I suppose Belcher is amongst them hidden anonymous - and Doctor Fettle in the background controlling with a walkie talkie set giving orders through it - here come the gas shells - watch out!

A thin mist spread amongst the patients - leaking from the canisters - and soon unaccountably they were laughing - was it laughing gas - that was kind of the authorities. Hedge collapses onto his hands and knees and found himself facing Shirley - what's in a name - hard to get his head round Margaret Emerson MI5 - she was giggling too...

I'm a gallon of Bonzo petrol woof woof ! WOOF WOOF ! Inspector Hedge was having the time of his life crawling around the lawn barking.

She joined in woof woof ! WOOF WOOF ! My God what a lark !

Soon the grounds were littered with the unconscious bodies of the patients who had stopped laughing and the staff moved in.

CHAPTER XXXIV

Later that afternoon - what was left of it - they were confined to a ward - keys jangling Belcher looking nervous - didn't want to be a part of it dear - not me - I'm on your side but what can you do - he who pays the piper calls the tune! Hedge in the ward now - deprived of his room was this a punishment - mixed ward this one eight beds and there was Shirley - he preferred to call her - across the aisle - and make of it what you could. Fragments of consciousness. They were dopey coming round from the effects of the laughing gas. Not likely to cause further trouble. He was in with the loons now. His cover could be his destruction - in too deep to get out - who was to calculate such matters? Next to him a burly patient gone to fat with worn lavatory brush facial hair midst which sat a bulbous red nose signalling warnings to passing ships - spoke up, Hello Major Johnson-Johnson, no need for formality. Have you been under yet?

What?

Down under? For whatever they do to one down there.

If I had would I know it?

Good point. Well I'm expecting to go down any time - for my part in the riots and no regrets - that will be the end of Major Johnson-Johnson as we know him today - Lord knows what sort of reconditioned creature I will emerge as - still loyal to Queen and Country I trust.

Who organised the riot? Asked Hedge.

It was the Patients Action Committee of which I am chairman - proudly I add. One serves as best one can on various boards - doing good - charitable work - but I am looking for a job - at the BBC I hope.

As a comedy producer?

No, as a doorman - but you've given me a good idea - a comedy producer yes.. Basically the BBC is a home to rehabilitate war veterans - other ranks doormen - comedy producers officers! Left wing sneaks go to drama! Nothing more to say - shutting up now.

Within the hour they came for the Major - injecting him into a coma - and there was the empty bed. And after that they came for Inspector Hedge - he was not injected but wheeled away in a chair. Shirley sitting on her bed - bedraggled hair looking like she'd just been dragged out of a lily pond where she had been floating after drowning herself - Ophelia - blew him a farewell raspberry. They took him to his room and left him there on his own. After a few minutes he got out of the wheelchair and crossed to the door. He tried the handle. It was locked. Hedge lay down upon his bed and stared at the kidney curtains...

I don't need to be told by that Major Johnson's Baby Powder excuse for a human being - an agent provocateur he is - getting the patients to riot so that the clinic could trial run its suppression techniques - trailing the laughing gas for the Government no doubt call it a side show if you like. They were putting on a lot of sideshows and they would like his case Code Name Green Swan to be one of them - he had been introduced - inserted - as a diversion - the Super had as good as told him that - yes he was a feint while the main attack went in somewhere else - the real investigation - whatever that was - into witchcraft - the dark arts yes practised by Defence - let's say Min of Defence - had got out of hand yes. So what was a small matter of a miscarriage of justice? A murder in an incurable ward - laugh it off - a mockery of justice - law and order - all he had been taught - Hedge - all he had believed in - that was now the sideshow - well was it? We would see - we would see about that - one good man could upset the apple cart - apples - one good apple in a rotten barrel...

He fell asleep.

Nurse Belcher was wheeling him down a corridor - as endless as such corridors were - him in a wheelchair blanket round his knees.

Don't believe that Major Johnson dear - he's been put up to it - stirring up the patients.

I worked that out already. Is this your ration of today's confidences Nurse Belcher?

Oh my don't you trust anyone? You're a hard one you are.

I'm working out whether I'm on a case or whether I just think I'm on a case. What do you think, Nurse? I know you're full of opinions facts and fancies.

And nursery tales my dear Inspector? There's so much that goes bump in the night, don't you find that?

I'm sure you do.

Oh! Thanks for that! I have no opinions, Inspector, lest they be scorned. My little advice to you dear - to pass the time no less and to be ignored - life is a corridor - is - is to live a little, dear. Today's the only one you've got. You think you should be somewhere else? With someone else? Doing something else? It's all here with little me.

Oh yes? That's interesting. Listen, you shot down my Doris - Mark One that is - Police property! Eh? What? Was that another diversion eh? To impede my enquiries? Were you following instructions from above?

Heaven knows dear! And here we are at last all merry and bright! We have suddenly arrived! Isn't that so true of life?

Nurse Belcher backed up the wheelchair and pushed open a door with her arse. The inspector was wheeled into an office where Doctor Fettle was waiting - his arse perched on his desk.

Inspector Hedge! Hello! That will be all Nurse.

Nurse Belcher retired.

Sorry about that demo you got caught up in Inspector. Never should have happened. Few troublemakers but then their neurotic sickness is something we should have anticipated. Any comments?

What?

Would you like to say anything?

Hedge stared at the doctor. Breathing. Breathing... the air in the room that belonged to the clinic. Ownership. That was the root of the problem. Don't own more than you can carry on the back of your horse.

The doctor picked up a file and opened it. Right. Well... we've been reviewing your case notes...

We?

Yes. How are you feeling? Any better?

How would I know? I was never aware that I was worse. In fact I don't see myself as a case - however many notes you've got.

I see. Good, yes...

The doctor stood up, moved behind his desk and sat down. He studied the inspector then looked away as if seeking inspiration before returning his gaze upon the man in the wheelchair.

Well... in that case you'll be glad to know that we consider you fit for discharge. How about you pack your things and leave tomorrow morning - after doctor's rounds - is that alright?

I came here on a case, Doctor Fettle. A case of my own. Not medical. A criminal investigation - you might care to recall.

Yes, I know you were under that illusion and I do not think that it serves your recovery to remain here. We are releasing you to care in the community.

Care? What? You think they care? The community? What community did you have in mind? Back at the Yard? It's a joke - a sick joke - what are you going on about? Community? Sniggers. People looking away. I did not receive a Get Well card from that lot - that's a fantasy! Am I being too sensitive? That is not the issue. I need this case solved to show them - to show them - yes - oh yes to show them what I can do - what I - what I am made of... I need - more than that - I need to do my duty.

Yes. That would be healing. To do your duty. You're talking about Code Name Green Swan I take it?

I am indeed. The Incurable Ward - down below - a germ warfare experiment gone wrong - gone awry - and you think you can fob me off with case notes? I've got case notes - don't you worry doctor - don't you worry about that - and they incriminate you. Listen, if you think I'm well then why would I be going on like this? If you think Code Name Green Swan is my illusion then I still have it - so how can you dream of letting me back into the community? And all the caring bastards out there?

The doctor studied his finger nails.

Well - put it this way - this place is closing down - within a month that is - least the public service part of it. It's not working with the security issues we are dealing with so we're going completely underground so to speak.

What will happen to the incurables ?

They'll be dead by then.

So what will the cover be for your operation?

It's going to easier to declare it a private government facility. Off limits to the Public. Should have done that all along, but...

But you needed members of the Public you could experiment on.

Whatever we needed that phase of the operation is being concluded. I'm sorry, Inspector, particularly as I was enjoying treating you.

You were in touch with my Super. You took me in to give me a cover story for my investigations.

No - I can't agree with that version of things - though it is noted in your records. It's hardly important in the light of your substantial recovery - which I trust will continue out in the Big Wide World where you belong, Inspector. Some of our patients are being shipped to other facilities in the NHS but I have not changed my opinion that you are better returned to the community on a different medication.

Is that what it's all about? Medication? Medical straight-jacket is it? Chuck him out - he's harmless! As long as he takes his medicine!

The doctor smiled. Quite. You have been suffering from some unfortunate side effects - as we've played along to find the correct dosage and the right meds best for you.

Side effects? That's what it is is it? Is that what it says on the bottle? You may imagine you are on a case, Inspector. It is real to you. There is nothing going on except in your mind.

It suits you to say that. You're feeling the heat. Say I refuse to leave?

That is not an option, Inspector. I'm sorry.

What's happening to Miss Emerson?

That's not your business. It's patient confidentiality. Let's get you out of here in the morning - you're going to feel a lot better believe me - out there. I don't want you becoming institutionalised.

I'm already in one institution - Scotland Yard.

Speaking of which I have a package here - from your Super.

The doctor placed a package onto the inspector's lap.

You won't get rid of me that easily. I know what's going on. We're closing in on you. Inspector Hedge stared the doctor down.

Very well. Belcher! Shouted Doctor Fettle.

Nurse Belcher immediately appeared. He must have been standing outside the door.

Take this patient back to his room, Nurse.

I could walk, said Hedge.

Don't bother dear - you'd be doing me out of a job. Off we go then!

Back in his room. On his own. What had Belcher said on the way back? Come to Evening Service. But where's the vicar? In the Incurable Ward. What had the vicar said that time? I am ordained in the Ancient Ministry before Christ who is one of our favourite sons - gay - beyond description male female, One...

Words. Do you get it? No. Come to the service, said Belcher. It will surprise you. Why would he, Jack - our Jack - waste the precious few hours he had left on the case in such a way? Could they force him to leave the clinic? Who was pulling the levers? Because Jack Hedge did not give up that easily. You've got the wrong number there...

He climbed out of the wheelchair. He opened the package. It contained an Inflatable Policewoman Mark 2 - the eyes upgraded to video record. Hedge blew her up and - consulting the manual - decided not to activate the camera yet - not to waste the battery that must be somewhere oh there it was rechargeable in the mains - never mind - he needed some time out - Maisie he decided to call her - Maisie with the prying eyes otherwise attractive I suppose - why put him and her together with so much stress on the case - they were bound to seek release.... Is that what they - whoever they were and feeling the heat - is that what they wanted? A means to break him? To compromise the inspector and remove him? As he was closing in for the kill...

He was crossing the grounds towards the chapel. Evening. Dark. Of course it got dark earlier - or later. Was it Spring or Autumn? Snow a few days ago? Sunshine - sweat - sort it out Inspector - the season., lad! Leaves on the trees whispering above his head. Make that Spring and work off the meds - exercise - don't give in. Still in one piece. He was winning. Other things to occupy him now...

Formed an attachment with Maisie and her hardly out of the box - not in the instruction manual that - not the same as Doris but Doris was gone wasn't she? Punctured - repaired - repair job OK but life moves on - last glimpsed re-inflated but so what - he had Maisie now don't feel guilty about it - it was all about guilt wasn't it? Losing the approval of the tribe was the biggest fear - not losing your life - the tribe came first - deep-rooted instinct - no individual survival without the tribe - but it was a big leap to the Nation State - to the Min of Defence and to Ernie in tins - specially stamped tins of corrupted Code Name Green Swan infected human flesh to be delivered to the Yanks - and what reciprocal favours were they offering the Brits? What horrors towards The Defence Of The Realm? Stop ! He shouldn't have taken her from the wrappings - Maisie - you know and pumped her up - they were alright to stick in police cars - from a distance they looked like the real thing. Real. How real is real? These days - it wasn't his idea - to give him rubber dolls as partners on a crime case! A case he had a few hours left to close before he was discharged but who said he was a patient? How had it come to that? He had arrived with the full authority of the law demanding the coopera-tion of all concerned - the hospital administration - a murder enquiry was under way - as far as he was concerned - despite their devious devices to disengage him from his work - what lay behind it there was still time to discover. The golden lights of the chapel beckoned. through the gloom. OK Belcher what's the surprise you have in store?

CHAPTER XXXV

The chapel.

Softly lit - the organ playing in the background - few people in for the service - took a while to make them out - shadows coming into focus. There was Sir Hilary Spong - up ahead in a pew the other side waving - recognition. Medical staff as per - as you would say - patients sprinkled - where was Miss Emerson of MI5? Shirley? Before he could make her out amongst the motley assembled - surely a few suits in tonight - spies - the Establishment turning up? Are the Ruskies back to feed the imagination? Well well, what's on? Is the balloon going up tonight?

Hello Hedge.

He turned to see beside him the Super - plain clothes - smartly dressed. That's how they got the top jobs - good dressers - he was already dressed for the next rank up - commissioner! Suit like that? Good clobber mate...

Sir?

Take this.

The Super pressed a revolver into his hands.

Armed response unit? Whispered Hedge. I haven't been trained for this, sir. I haven't been on the range for years.

You know how to pull the bloody trigger don't you? Push forward the safety catch and point the thing in the direction of perceived threat. Bang! You're dead.

Right. Hedge slipped the gun into his dressing gown pocket. Underneath he was wearing a pair of hospital pyjamas - his clothes had been removed since the demo - same with all the patients.

I'm being released into the care of the community tomorrow, whispered Hedge.

My arse you are. Concentrate on the case. We've got the heavies in.

The suits?

They want the glory. It's our case Hedge. Shape up Inspector. You could be stepping up the ladder tonight. It depends how you perform.

The organ music swelled and soon they were standing and singing the hymn All Things Bright And Beautiful. There was Shirley! Had she just come in - behind him - singing sweetly in her hospital pyjamas. Now she was real - that's where the problems start.

The hymn finished during which had entered a figure in vestments. Portly - well not quite gone to fat - Belcher - that damn queer bloke - odd - trying to get a grasp on his affections no way - no way Jose! He had to reorientate he knew that - homophobia was out - it was a love-in now in the Force - my God took some getting used to - careful what you say son - no more entrapments in the toilets - they teach you one thing then tell you you've got to forget it - all in a lifetime - all in a service career - but they don't know what's going on inside your head, do they? So what has the lovely gay Belcher to say - all dressed up in his robes - and we know where the Vicar is - dying off in the Incurable Ward with all the other unfortunate wretches - though one of 'em could be a murderer laughing at justice to pass the time.

Belcher was speaking...

It is my privilege to address you this evening - the previous incumbent has at last and not before time been removed for apostasy. He is with that number of clerics who renounce the Old Religion - imagining that they can go forward when they need to go back to the Old Truths - indeed the Eternal Truths - that were on Salisbury Plain at Stonehenge revealed to our ancestors on a summer solstice. We were promised visitors from another world to help us against wickedness. Jesus is such a visitor - our favoured son - the Light to banish evil that seeks to overwhelm this land and to fulfil its promise made millennias ago that though the devil and his minions would return and seek to win the day - cast out as they were for the sins of pride - at the last trump they would be defeated. I hope that's not too much for your tiny minds to take in - do wake up at the back!

The congregation stirred with laughter and relief to be excused from deep thought.

Now, this evening we are to rejoice in a new addition to our church - not a false idol but a doll nevertheless I do confess. Let us name her Saint Agnes! No, possibly not. Well something else - original - importantly we may bring our worries to her feet and leave the burden of them with her - arising to go free about our daily business...

The organ started playing as a curtain was unveiled revealing the In-flated Policewoman Mark 1 - Doris. Picking up from their pews the hymn sheets prepared for them the congregation joined in singing,

All Saints are spirit, gone the blubber
Now we have one made of rubber!
Though it perishes it's true,
With the Saints we trust in you!

Are you Agnes? Are you Maisie?
Are you Doris? Are you Daisy?
Of your name we remain hazy
Let this not be as we're lazy...
For of your works we sing forever!
So let us call you our Saint Heather!
Heather on the Moor and wild,
Saint Heather bless us, old and child!
Saint Heather bless us, meek and mild!
Saint Heather, not with us the blubber
You are alone bless'd Saint in rubber!

We can't have that Hedge, hissed the Super. That's a desecration of one of our policewomen. I put her into your care - you were the senior partner - it was her first case.

I thought she was lost.

Lost?

Irretrievably. Gone.

That's why we sent you another police doll. I expect she's inflated lying in bed back in your room.

Hedge did not deny this.

We can't have this. Take your gun and shoot her down, Inspector.

Who?

You know who.

But...

No buts - you're on the job man - that's an order - take her down.

Inspector Hedge took out the revolver that had so recently been placed in his care by the Super. The congregation were still lustily singing when the shots rang out - One! Two! And the recently sanctified St Heather nee Policewoman Doris sagged shrank and collapsed...

He did it! Shouted the Super, grappling with Hedge. This madman over here! Here's your assassin!

At the same time while wrestling his bewildered inspector to the ground he whispered, Cooperate damn you - they won't discharge you into the community tomorrow on this showing - it would be scandalous. I need you deeper in. Pull the trigger! Point at the ceiling...

The Super pressed Hedges finger on the trigger of the revolver and another shot rang out taking off some plasterwork above.

I'VE GOT HIM! HELP! Yelled the Super. BEFORE HE KILLS SOMEONE!

Others joined in wrestling Inspector Hedge to the floor. Burly nurses fetched a straight-jacket. He was strapped up and carted off. The last words he heard before he was injected with a sedative - nestling in his ear comfortingly - was an encouraging aside from his superior, Well done Inspector.

CHAPTER XXXVI

Inspector Hedge opened his eyes and blinked several times. He saw that he was back in the underground park. He was seated in a canvas sling chair and opposite him across the table was seated Sir Hilary Spong.

Ah you're back with us Jack! May I call you Jack? Hilary here! Of course you know me - as well as you can know anyone in this godforsaken place that is. Yet here is pleasant enough wouldn't you say - a refuge - an eco-bubble, let's call it that - yes...

Elephants with swaying trunks were grazing nearby.

The thought is - and it all begins with a thought doesn't it - that's how the world began - that's scientific! Science and mysticism are coming together - because we are inventing an unknown world - we're making up the world as we go along - it's a matter of conjecture - there's nothing without us and our thought of it! The thought is that we create eco-bubbles in various parts of the world as a - a what? Hello, look at that big fellow - elephant! Beautiful creatures - be sure no-one will be experimenting on them - I'll make sure of that - twaddle! Balderdash! Where was I? Oh yes - these eco bubbles are like Noah's Ark - a series of them - we are saving what we can - in case the plague - nay the seven plagues! Come to decimate the earth. And that's what that wretched vicar fellow was about - yes, and I'll tell you why - as we're on the subject - his wild fevered brain imagined that if he could be party to releasing a devastating plague upon the country - what? Yes, all of that - and then he could call the Nation to repentance and save his religion from redundancy and complete irrelevancy! Of course he was being used in his turn...

Blimey, said Hedge. I've been nobbled again.

Sir Hilary chuckled. That's a good phrase! Nobbled! I like that, yes - he's been nobbled! How else could I get you here? And save you from worse. Have some cordial old chap - you must drink plenty of fluids.

Sir Hilary poured Hedge a drink from a jug of cordial. Hedge drank up.

Have some more. Sir Hilary refilled the glass.

I have some news for you. I don't know if it will come as a surprise. Your Superintendent is not on your side. He's one of them.

Them?

Yes, he's not one of us - isn't that obvious?

Hedge said, I'm not sure - I'm not sure whether this is a hallucination - every time they pump me up with drugs I finish up here.

Don't be damn silly, Inspector. Your Superintendent is one with the forces of evil...the forces of evil...the forces of evil...

The words echoed round Hedge's head as the scene went in and out of focus.

Come back to me Jack.

What?

You're a good 'un. I want you here.

The focus cleared. He stared at the specialist in God knows what - Sir Hilary Spong. Slap my face, he said.

What?

Slap my face hard.

If you insist.

Sir Hilary leant across the table and slapped the inspector's face.

Harder than that.

Sir Hilary hit him harder.

Right - right - OK then - I'm here... Inspector Hedge stood up. I'm bloody well here, aren't I? On a case...

He collapsed across the table - Blackout.

He was in his room - his kidney motif-style room - and she - Stella / Maureen / Angela - what the hell was your name? Who are you? He shouted at the inflatable policewoman Mark Two. Got a camera have you? All switched on is it? Taking it all in? Are you? Gladys? What's in a name? Well listen I killed for you - a previous lover - Doris - eh? Policewoman Doris...Listen I punctured her good and proper - two shots I'm sure - not worth repairing - she's redundant gone - only did still shots of the crime scene Doris - farewell Doris..

He was staggering about the room trying to keep his feet - like a drunk but no drink had passed his lips - they'd shot him up with something. He collapsed into a chair. Listen Maisie - alright I remember - Maisie - it's a mugs game Maisie - one blow up doll is much like another - if you ask me that is - and who is asking me? No-one - because I am on my own Inflatable Policewoman Mark Two Maisie - you have no character except I invent it - but I Maisie - I Maisie - would like - very much - to invent the character of a real person - like Miss Emerson - or Shirley - and start a detective agency with her right? Not you you rubber monstrosity - you accountants answer to a staff shortage - come here! Come on let's make the best of it. He stood up and crossed to the bed and pulled the inflatable policewoman off the bed into his arms and started cavorting round the room singing his own song in his own copyright secure,

Oh my dear Inflatable you
You might be unreal but to me you are true
Don't leave me and float out into the blue
For without angel wings I can't follow you...
Our love is divine through hope and despair
If you puncture my dreams they're beyond repair
If this be sweet love what know I about it?
Thank God that you came with a puncture repair outfit...
Oh my Inflatable!
My own inescapable!
Always so datable!
Though you're made of rubber you're totally mate-able...
You...!

He collapsed onto the floor on top of the doll, slobbering, laughing...

Well we're ready Maisie ain't we - we're ready yes - we're ready to be released - haha - released into the care of the community.

Ha ha said the clown.

CHAPTER XXXVII

She said hurry. They were walking along a corridor - one of those endless corridors - she had hold of his hand - you're alright she said. Doors were closed - when one door closes another opens - who said that - a door manufacturer no doubt. Come on she said - keep up - we're getting out of here...

My case.

Fuck your case!

A door was open - light spilled into the shadows of the corridor promising what? Engagement. Inspector Hedge burst into an office and she had gone.

There you are said Doctor Fettle seated languidly behind his desk. Do sit down Inspector.

Hedge sat down breathing heavily. He looked at Fettle searching his face for answers.

Fettle said well...

Hedge - getting a second wind - well?

I expect you would like an update Inspector.

He was an inspector now. Was he getting cooperation? At last?

It's like this. I'm so sorry you had to be sedated - and so heavily - that was careless - just as you were getting well - just as we had a discharge date for you tomorrow - and now that's been set back - though I don't blame you. CTV evidence shows that you were got at - provoked - so you're still on the case for a little while - a little longer what?

Doctor Fettle smiled reassuringly.

You mean I'm not ill?

That was a cover - we both know that - but I had to play the game. I've got some bad news I'm afraid - Sir Hilary Spong has suffered a mishap.

As you know this is a dangerous - what shall we say - assignment? Case? Yes - case - for us the medical profession to become involved in and it calls into question our very own ethics - oh yes we have them. Security? National security? How far down the road does that take us? Until we are hopelessly compromised - all bearings gone - lost - and corrupted. My God I'm aware of that but Sir Hilary had entered another plane - when that happened I know not - what day what hour there was no longer the possibility of retreat - to decency? His title gave him a certain self-justification - an awful pride hidden as an easy going modesty that could fool anyone. You'd better come with me Inspector. Pride comes before a fall - I'm afraid that is very true.

In the lift going down Inspector Hedge had a strong hunch where he would find Sir Hilary Spong. And so it turned out to be. A few minutes later through the observation window of the Incurable Ward he saw the Knight of the Realm in a bed a saline drip plugged into his arm.

I was with him not so long ago in the underground park, said Hedge. How come he finished up in here?

He insisted upon entering the ward, explained Doctor Fettle. Apparently there was an emergency.

An emergency? What sort of emergency?

The vicar had had a fit - he was frothing at the mouth - that's the last stage of this disease - this dreadful disease.

But the vicar was a newcomer.

That's interesting, yes. They can go suddenly to the latter stages of this terrible illness...

Code Name Green Swan, muttered Hedge.

Precisely. We think it's a cocktail of plague viruses. They are not sure themselves what they have cooked up - created in their Hell's Kitchen.

Created? Who are they?

The scientists of course. Who fell victim to their own madness. They are all in there. Young Alan Harbour - Fletcher, very clever man - Morgan - Heartfelt absent, in the morgue.

Where's the vicar?

He's with George Heartfelt. The team leader. In the morgue. He succumbed the same day.

I see. Why did Sir Hilary go into the Incurable Ward?

I dare say he had his own reasons.

You don't know?

I don't know why he had to go in there.

Let's put it another way - what stopped him leaving?

He was in the decontamination chamber to come out when the alarm went off. He had picked up the bug. Perhaps it was in the air. Mutating. No-one can go in there now. Not even you Inspector. Your case must remain unsolved.

Belcher appeared.

The new regulations are in force Doctor, he said.

How did you get the corpses out? Hedge continued to interrogate the doctor.

Belcher butted in. With difficulty luv - total decontamination suit - like the one they used on the moon - interior air supply - high oxygen content darling - it's a gas! Wow!

It reduces communication rather than enhancing it. There is absolutely no point in you entering that ward wearing one of those suits, insisted the doctor.

Hedge was absorbing information. Or misinformation. Getting a feel of it. Quickly. No time to waste now. Things were coming to a head. I need to ask Sir Hilary Spong a few questions, he said.. I notice even from here that there are signs of bruising on his head.

He fell over, said Fettle. Getting into bed - the shock to the system can make one giddy - not really believing you could catch it - even with all your knowledge something else takes over - there's a gambler in all of us - and one day you decide to chance it! Perhaps he was unhappy about something at home and that made him rash. We are emotional creatures more than rational beings, Inspector.

I need to talk to him - through the communication system, ordered Hedge.

No problem, said the doctor. We'll call him over. Flag him - if he's well enough to get out of bed.

It's broken, said Belcher. The communications are down.

How come, Nurse? Fettle sounded indignant.

Something put on for his benefit? Another charade guessed Hedge.

We've called the engineers, said Belcher. It's no good getting your knickers in a twist, Doctor. Shit happens - especially when it's full moon tomorrow.

I want this fixed NOW ! Stormed Doctor Fettle. It's the only way we can get through to them. Because nobody's going in that ward from now on - except with moon suits to remove dead bodies! GOT IT? Is that clear?

Clear as the nose on your face, Doctor Fettle. Belcher curtsied and said with a loud aside to the inspector, I don't take to bullying in the workplace. You are my witness to that. If I need one.

No-one! Absolutely no-one is to go into that ward! Doctor Fettle shouted. I repeat - they can do their own chores - they can make their own beds - and they can die off the sooner the better - and we'll shut this blasted wing down.

Doctor Fettle turned on his heels and walked away, disappearing into the lift.

That outburst had the ring of sincerity, don't you agree Inspector? Said Belcher. I suggest you go and have some supper, dear. It's only regular meals that makes life tolerable in this dump.

It's tantamount to murder - whoever put Sir Hilary in there, said Hedge. He never fell over to get that bruise.

Don't expect me to stray from the official version darling.

Let me know as soon as the communicating device through to the ward is repaired, instructed Hedge. I need to talk to Sir Hilary Spong as a matter of urgency.

Alright. Though you might do better to learn semaphore - or tapping on pipes, dear! There are people here who won't want you communicating with the dead.

They're still alive Nurse.

Do you think there's much difference?.

CHAPTER XXXVIII

He stared down at a plate of macaroni cheese searching in its shape and patterns for inspiration - but none came. There was a clunk as another plate of macaroni cheese joined him at the table and Shirley sat down opposite him.

Usual shit, she said. Fit for pigs ain't it?

Inspector Hedge raised his eyes from the plate to look her in the face. Who are you? Are you a patient here pretending to be Miss Emerson of MI5? Or are you Miss Emerson pretending to be a barmy patient?

Wot's it to you mate? She stuck a fork into a piece of macaroni, put it in her mouth and chewed. It's a matter of staying alive in't it? That's why we eat this crap.

It's safe to talk, suggested Hedge quietly.

Since when mate?

I mean - put it another way - you're human aren't you? Flesh and blood - it's always going to be difficult - communicating like - you know what I mean.

She chewed on her macaroni. Got to keep it down mate - it's nourishment, in't it?

Hedge watched her masticating, trying to break through to the truth. You could give me a sign. These have been disturbing days - if we cross-reference each other we may stay sane. He stuck his fork in the gooey mess but did not lift it to his mouth. Look at it this way - I've had enough - I'm up to here with it - early retirement? I'm taking it - after this case I tell you - start a little detective agency and whoever you are - you're in. Can't say fairer than that - I'm going out on a limb making you an offer.

She stared at him then spat a mouthful of gob onto the floor. Look mate, she said and added in a voice he had heard before - cultivated - money spent on an education... Be repulsed by my table manners.

What?

She went on masticating. Mate! She shouted. One thing! One thing mate! I am shag-worthy! Face that! Give me respect mate!

Of course yes...

We are citizens of the world mate! Do you realise how much they trust us 'ere? Giving us knives and forks like? Wot? Eh? Mate? All this fucking cutlery? In fucking metal mate! Not pissing plastic! We could do serious damage with these weapons! If we so chose...

A male nurse on dining room duty was keeping watch on what could turn into an incident though he hoped not to have to write it up. Not another strait-jacket job he hoped - he wanted to get home early tonight.

You're disgusting, said Hedge loudly.

She murmured, Find a way to get into the grounds tonight. Very Oxford. Degree English Lit. Then more...

Fuck you mister! Shit for brains you are! A walking penis you are! Do you know that? You stay out of my sight mate or I'll have your fucking bollocks off! She stood up pushed the table at him and walked out of the dining room shouting, You want it you know where to come don't yer?! I'm the local nympho can't help me-self can I?! It's in me medical records! Look for yourself! Fuck for England I do! You should be proud of me! Anything you like! Get it up - that's my motto! Pathetic lot of fucking twots you lot are! You don't know what your 'oles are for! You make me vomit!

The male nurse laughed as she walked out. Nothing out of the ordinary tonight. Get home - open a tin of corned beef.

Inspector Hedge stood up. He slipped a knife up his sleeve and left the dining room.

CHAPTER XXXIX

Damn you Maisie! Switched on are you? Remote control is it? The eyes of the rubber doll Inflatable Policewoman Mark Two Maisie - so named - seemed to be burning - boring holes into Inspector Hedge's skull. It's not working Maisie - it's different - it's over - you got me on the rebound - made of rubber you'd know all about that - plenty of bounce in you Maisie haha. Point is it's no sort of relationship - I'm talking to myself - the magic has gone - I had that with Doris - your predecessor - for a while we had something but it's asking a lot mixing work with personal relationships - especially in our sort of trade - detection. Bloody accountants - how much do they save on manpower with the dolls? No pensions to start with - no days off sick - puncture repair outfit and you're ready to go.

The doll seemed to be nodding - sat upon the bed. Hedge took out the knife.

I took this knife to stab you but - it would be damaging police property wouldn't it? And deducted from my already insufficient salary - not that I have a lot of expenses - I don't drink smoke or gamble so I put a bit by - never enough is it Maisie? No it ain't - or no it is not... Listen - listen to the wind. Is it air escaping from you Maisie? Have you sprung a leak? Are you like the Hindenburg Zeppelin about to explode? Depends how you're pumped up - how much can you take? How much inflation? Before the bubble bursts? It's all economics isn't it?

He stood up...

I must go. Night has fallen and it's taking no prisoners. I'm out of here Maisie - back to the Yard to hand in my resignation - I've been used shamelessly - by the Big Boys who don't care - to them I'm just a number - every policeman has got a number. These are the last hours - if I can get some resolution - Code Name Green Swan - I'll do it - I'll solve the case and throw it in their faces - you know the pigs - the filth - you know all about them. These are the last minutes Maisie and I can't take you with me - I won't deflate you and pack you away - I'll let you take your chances... Basically Maisie let's face it - it's not your fault - it's not our fault - it's all about surviving - which mean getting an identity - and I've given you one - it's authentic so make the best if it Maisie Bye Bye.

The Inspector went to the door and tried it. It was locked. He had the knife and he forced the blade into the door jamb and sprang the lock. He opened the door and left the kidney motif curtains and the rocking doll of dreams - dreams that people real people would not let you realise.

In the grounds he took a deep breath and smelt the earth and felt the heat of the day in the earth - yet he had come here mid-winter - or possibly not - hard to tell - summer days yet snow somewhere - or had he been here longer than he figured? It was dark now and he was drawn to a thumping noise of machinery like the bass notes of a rock concert - and lights flung against the trees - background shadows as if nature was witnessing another plundering of its resources - a derrick drilling into the soil that contained more than the nutrients of life - below were the layers of conspiracy and murder.

How long had he been here?

Snow?

Outside the window at Scotland Yard?

He was already on medication before he arrived at the clinic. Inspector Hedge was his name. The case was rooted in a blasphemy against nature, that much he had discovered. Mother Earth forgive us for we have sinned.

Hello Hedge!

It was the Super - on the edge of the lit area as the drill thumped and twisted downward. Shadowy figures of workers in hard hats attended the machinery - Village People cue for song YMCA!

Pay attention Hedge - our story comes to a climax.

Story sir?

Every case is a story, that's why we're continually fictionalised. Turned into heroes or scum. You've done well Inspector - in both roles - but this thing is bigger than both of us. You're off the case, it's been suspended - well let's say abandoned.

Abandoned?

Lack of evidence - we could not go to trial on what we know - the Director of Prosecutions is redirecting our resources.

But...

No buts, Hedge. This is it. We have a licence to explore this ground - we're drilling for oil.

That's a cover if ever I heard one, said Hedge. You're drilling for elephants. He laughed.

You're not well - or that's your role - whatever you're doing, Inspector, it's played out. Other forces have taken over. Pack your stuff - you're being discharged in the morning.

I thought you wanted me more deeply embedded?

It doesn't matter what I want anymore. You're on convalescent leave and outpatient therapy.

Where?

How the hell should I know?

I'm not coming back here as an outpatient?

Nobody is. The NHS contract is cancelled.

But we in the Force have private insurance...

Don't complicate my life, Hedge. It's over. Finito. Got it? Now get out of my sight, there's a good chap. I've got work to do.

Hedge turned away and wandered off. You couldn't finish a case like this - the incurables - the murder - framed in a darker conspiracy for sure - one thing leading to another - it was starting to unravel and then they call the whole ruddy thing off? Not on my watch mate! There's such a thing as job satisfaction and I mean to have it - oh yes - grammar school that's me - scholarship boy! The idea was the best could come up out of the masses so to speak - from the working classes you get it? And enrich the economy - that was the idea - social engineering mate! But when they did that - Them - Them, oh yes - They bit off more than they could chew din't they - cos he could - oh yes he could - he could take on The Establishment - if he had to. He wasn't finished with this case - not with his credentials - they'd be laughing the other side of their faces before he was finished. Oh yes...

Inspector Hedge walked round the dark building of the clinic and saw across the shadowed grounds another pool of light. Was this another oil rig night drilling?

He came closer and saw that a crane was lifting a crate out of the earth and he heard the sound of an elephant trumpeting. So that was it - they were vacating the underground park. Getting rid of the animals as well as the patients. Were these two night operations working in conjunction with each other? Or did different agencies with different agendas simply get on with doing their own thing? After all this was England. Nobody had to know what anybody else was doing.

He saw her in the trees, a flitting shadow. Miss Emerson. Or Shirley. There was a construction. A shed she was heading for. She pushed open the door and disappeared inside. He followed, carefully pushing open the hanging door, praying it would not creak. It did. From the deep shadows that configured garden machinery, she spoke,

You want to know what's going on, don't you Jack? Time to get intimate, darling and share a few secrets. It was her Oxford voice.

He moved towards her and his eyes became accustomed to the gloom so that he could make out her movements. She had rolled up the sleeve of her blouse. She took out a cord or a piece of material and tied it as a tourniquet around her arm. She took out a syringe...

Hang on, Miss Emerson. We don't self medicate on the job.

Yes we bloody well do. Or else my education would be entirely useless. I got a First at Magdalen in getting wasted.

She plunged the needle into her upper arm and emptied the contents of the syringe. She threw it aside, released the tourniquet and waited for the rush. When it came she sighed contentedly.

Right, I'm all yours. On with the motley, she added in a deliberately funny voice

Miss Emerson, I cannot condone this behaviour. It could impair your judgement.

The opposite is true, Dumbo. I can see for miles and miles and miles. Come on.

She left the shed. Inspector Hedge had little choice but to follow.

Were you placed in this clinic to detox? He demanded as he stumbled along behind her.

I needed a cover story, darling.

Is that what you call it? That's ripe.

Shut up, she hissed from the darkness. Keeping well away from the pools of light and the security men looming in and out of the night Miss Emerson led the way towards the back of the main clinic building. She found a door that opened to her touch and entered. They were in a corridor. Hedge thought that the clinic was more a series of corridors than rooms or facilities - that the whole establishment had been built to provide corridors in the first place rather like the BBC TV Centre and that the other uses of the building were an afterthought. After all corridors and tea trolley meetings were where it all happened.

Hang on, he said. Look, it's my job to find out what's really going on in this maze of corridors. I am conducting an investigation. Whoever you are - what? Whoever you think you may be - that is really beside the point.

Oh really? Her eyes were like bright pins reflecting the moon. Though where was the moon?

She turned on him and grabbed his collar. What do you know about what is real? You fucking plod? The only thing that's going to save us tonight is an act of imagination.

I want the facts...

There's no such thing as facts, idiot. We are into post quantum physics. There are no facts without an observer and an observer can only find what he is already looking for - the rest passes him by - which is most of the fucking Universe! So do me a favour and get in the fucking lift will you?

Alright. No need to get shirty, Miss. I can't see you paying back your student loan. Actually, I don't know which is which but I prefer your other persona.

They got into the lift and she pressed descend.

You can't carry on like this you know, he said - taking drugs like Sherlock Holmes - looking for inspiration.

I see connections that others don't darling, she said - her of the pinned eyes - breathing she was heavily - deeply - wild - not a lady more a witch. Oh Jack love me for the sake of love, don't be such a dull plodder, it is no coincidence we have come together - do you think the agencies are managing this? They are beyond help - they are being used.

Come on, growled Hedge. What's your name? What is your name now? Who the hell are you? What's made up? Tell me. Be frank and we can get somewhere.

Poor Jack, she said and kissed him lightly. Cling to the wreckage - help is coming.

The lift pinged as the doors opened. They were met by a frantic Belcher.

Oh Gawd it's a full evacuation! So it is! Who knows why cos I don't dear! The fear is in them for sure - Them Upstairs have decided! To close the whole lot down! And we must do what we must do, mustn't we? The script is writ and we must play our parts, tralaa! Well it makes a day I say - who'd have it any other way?

What's the status of the Incurables, Belcher? demanded Miss Emerson.

Poorly, to be sure, Miss.

The metal shutter was down. Hedge turned on the nurse.

How can you evacuate those creatures highly infected as they are? That's not so easy, is it? What's to be done with them? There's a case here Belcher to be answered - Nurse I must enter that ward - I will not be deterred, you hear me?

Steady Jack, we're all on the same side here, Joyce Emerson soothed him.

Belcher fluttered a wrist towards the Inspector. We're too late, luv.

Do you think they'll let you rescue anything out of this? That's not the plan, is it?

I'm going in, shouted Hedge. Raise the shutter! This time nothing will stop me. Justice will be done you hear? It won't be mocked.

Oh listen to him! It does your heart good, simpered Belcher. So macho, I'm getting goose bumps.

Raise the shutter, ordered Hedge. And if you have a decontamination suit I am minded to put it on.

Joyce flopped down in a chair. Oh my God what a farce. Let it play out Belcher, do as he says.

Yes your Majesty, said Belcher with a curtsy and pressed a button. The shutter began to ascend.

Inspector Hedge took note. Inside the ward there was a glimpse of normal life - call it normal - Sir Hilary Spong abed a drip feed to his arm - the vicar removed gone to the morgue, a sense of absence of the vicar - and there was Morgan sitting on his bed reading a magazine - Fletcher doing press ups on the floor - and young what's his name? Hudson? No - whoever he was he was sitting at a table doing a jigsaw puzzle. These were the scientists gone missing in the hardly reported plane disappearance - the three of them plus chopped up Ernie - or minced in tins - yet the informants were within - he must interrogate them - that was his job and nothing would stop him this time.

Forget the space suit, lad. I could not conduct my enquiries properly in that.

Oh I can't let you take the risk without it, said Nurse Belcher. I'm just getting to know you and suddenly you're gone, Inspector? I don't take to people that easily. You might consider the feelings of others for a change.

What was that gay fairy faggot going on about? He liked him well enough - don't come too close - mind you we could do without the emotion.

Stop that Belcher - an officer in carrying out his duties cannot shilly shally. I'm going in.

It's true, said Joyce Whoever She Was, he can't cross examine people in that ridiculous suit. He might as well be on the moon. But look what happened to the vicar? He went in on faith alone to that ward...

No, he was chucked in unconscious last time, said Belcher.

Never mind that, said Hedge. Time's passing. I've got a hunch this is my last chance to make a meaningful enquiry and I mean to make the most of it.

Say something to stop him, begged Belcher.

Oh what the fuck darling, said Miss Emerson. What's one copper more or less. He's a pig and he's pigheaded! So go ahead and die.

It's a balanced risk, Hedge replied. He was at the door of the chamber.

I'm glad you think so. Belcher's right actually. There are people that care about you - more fool them.

And I care about my duty, said Hedge. Somebody's got to do it.

He laid hands upon the wheel to spin it and unlock the outer door of the chamber. As he did so a red light above the door flashed on and off and a siren harshly hooted, clattering their ears.

Request denied, shouted Belcher above the din. You can't get in.

Why the hell not? Inspector Hedge was shouting back. As he stared into the incurable ward a drill burst through the roof and water poured in. The siren stopped. The light above the door stayed red.

That's why dear, said Belcher. It's in lockdown. No-one in, no-one out.

Where's that water coming from? Hedge stared in horror at the scene.

The swimming pool darling.

They watched through the observation window as the ward filled up like a gold fish bowl. The incurables were floating with the furniture. Hedge grabbed a fire extinguisher and smashed it against the window but it only bounced off.

We can't just let them drown, he said.

That's what they're doing, said Joyce Emerson.

Fletcher swam along the observation window. Sir Hilary was already face down on the surface - Hudson no that's not his name was going down for the third time - and Morgan was atop a table. Still the water was rising - rising to the ceiling of the ward forcing Morgan off the table to struggle in the water of this B-movie death trap.

Seen enough, have you dear? Belcher pressed a button and the shutter silently descended, closing out the scene.

We're done here, said Joyce. Come on.

The bastards were drilling down to do that! Hedge was raving. To drown the incurables! They knew what they were doing. Destroying the evidence weren't they? It's all going in my report. Someone's going to pay for this!

Do you think anyone's going to listen to you? You're a looney who's had a nervous breakdown, remember? She took his arm.

Hedge stared at the woman - who was she? Who was he? Did it matter any more?

I'm handing in my resignation first thing Monday morning, said Inspector Hedge.

They turned away from the scene of desolation, defeated and demoralised. As they were leaving the precinct of the incurable ward for the last time Nurse Belcher remarked,

I think we should open a detective agency. Just the three of us. Speaking for myself I've had it up to here with the NHS...

Out of the earth they came - the three of them - climbing the emergency stairs to exit into the startled night where all was clamour and dazzling lights and shouted orders and backing lorries and the braying of elephants.

What was to be done?

Inspector Hedge and Margaret Emerson come Shirley what's in a name and the the objectionable Belcher who had won a place in the scheme of things walked away into the silence of the moon-bathed countryside. And as they walked the sound of pipe and drum carried to them. And they were part of the French Grand Armée leaving Waterloo following their Field Marshal Napoleon who was on horseback. Towards the dawning sky they marched carrying their colours that would rise another day on another field of battle. How narrow can be the understanding between victory and defeat. And Belcher it was in torn blue private's uniform who spun that brave tune through a pipe. Beside him marched Shirley the determined lad whose tears glistened in the morning rays of sun as she beat a drum. And Jack Hedge marched in that procession of beaten soldiers and camp followers carrying in his arms a newborn babe that softly mewled. There was always new life. Everything would begin again and in new roles they would love and play and suffer together. For the stories are endless.

www.ingramcontent.com/pod-product-compliance
Lightning Source LLC
Chambersburg PA
CBHW061522020726
47502CB00006B/2186